THE
HEALER
AND THE
WARLORD

To the healers.

Author's Note

This book is a fantasy romance intended for adults. As such, it contains heavy themes and intense action typical of the genre, as well as on-page physical intimacy.

If you like your stakes high and your romance sizzling, this book is for you!

CHAPTER ONE

KELVAR

T he night was quiet, but my mind was not. The warm air was disturbed only by the gentle snort of my horse behind me and the vibrating strings of magic attaching me to every living thing in the Ballan desert.

Dileas gently bumped her head against my back, as if the mare was asking what I was waiting for. After all, the sooner I fulfilled the wishes of Lord Deryn, the sooner we could gallop across the moonlit sands again.

I closed my eyes, homing in on the warmth of my horse's breath puffing through my light linen tunic, grounding my focus. When we were riding together, sometimes I imagined my consciousness fracturing out to cover the entire desert, the magic within me stretching my awareness impossibly far from the mountains in the east to the ocean in the west. Now though, I needed to focus. The desert's magic could help me achieve my task if I could but master it.

And master it I would.

Flickering flames of life, all concentrated in a patch not far away, appeared in my mind's eye. I wasn't far from Clan Padra's encampment.

With a gentle pat on Dileas's nose telling her to stay put, I started off across the dunes. The soft leather soles of my boots swished against the sands, indistinguishable from the wind to those who weren't listening closely.

Ahead, the shadows of a city of tents rose out of the darkness. Small structures, big enough for just a single rider, formed concentric circles around larger and larger dwellings, with a tall peak at the center adorned with a dark banner, swaying lazily in the breeze.

Tonight was a new moon, making it dark enough that I couldn't make out the symbol on the banner, but I knew it to be the maroon scorpion of Clan Padra. It marked the tent where the Lord slept.

And where I would find his daughter.

I reached the edge of the encampment, slipping by an enclosed paddock where horses snorted sleepily. I pulled my power around myself like a cloak, letting it shield me from the eyes of any clansmen who might be wandering about at night, but the horses still saw me. The desert's magic was strong enough in the beasts that they would not be fooled by such a simple trick. Still, they did not see me as a threat, as I projected calm and admiration in their direction. They let me slip by with no commotion.

I padded through the camp like a wraith, quickly making my way from the small tents of single riders to the larger dwellings that would hold families. I hadn't been to this encampment before, but they were all laid out the same. My own small shelter was always on the fringes of Clan Katal's encampment, as close to the pasture where Dileas slept as possible. I was often called to the Lord's tent at the very center to advise him on battle plans or to be sent on some mission, though.

The only noises that drifted out from behind tent flaps were gentle snores and the occasional whisper of a couple who thought they were unobserved, murmuring promises to each other in the privacy of a moonless night.

My lip curled in distaste. I didn't enjoy missions like this, creeping through the shadows unseen. I wished for a horse between my thighs and the thrill of bloodlust to drive the whispers of the desert's magic from my mind. My power was better suited to calling down storms than stealth. But this was what Lord Deryn had demanded of me, and I always did as he ordered. He was the only family I had, after all.

As I reached the largest tent in the encampment, I paused. My palms hovered an inch from the canvas wall at the rear of the structure, not touching it yet as I took a deep, steadying breath. The air tasted of sunbaked earth, undercut by something metallic and familiar: Magic.

A shudder climbed up my spine, and I frowned at the reaction.

Magic was not foreign to me, often pouring off my own skin in inexorable waves that unnerved those around me. It wasn't uncommon for clan lords to also carry significant power, as the nine clans of the Ballan desert only suffered to be ruled by the strong.

The taste coating my tongue as I breathed, though, was strange—not what I would expect of a warrior who had gained the respect of Clan Padra's riders. It was less metallic—sweeter—as if it called out to me through the thin barrier before me.

Its pull grew in my mind until I couldn't help but rest my palms on the tent wall in front of me. I leaned in to rest my cheek on the coarse canvas as well, subconsciously listening for signs of life inside.

Instead of the heavy texture of roughspun I expected, the fabric gave way, like the lightest of linens, woven by the finest craftsmen of the desert. It was as if the call of magic inside the dwelling had grown so inexorable, physical barriers had become ephemeral and inconsequential in the face of its strength.

I raised my eyebrows and my lips quirked. Slowly, I pushed my hands forward. They sank through the canvas as if it were water, only a sensation like sand on the breeze signaling that I passed through a formerly solid object.

I stepped through the canvas and exhaled quietly through my nose in surprise, as I found myself standing in the quiet dark of the Lord's tent. I had never been able to walk through solid objects before, and a thrill ran from the top of my head to the soles of my boots at the thought. The desert had her own agenda and occasionally seemed to bestow me with new abilities depending on her whims. What her goals were, though, I had never been able to decipher.

I squeezed my eyes shut in the quiet tent, waiting for a wave of chattering voices to pass through my consciousness, as they so often did when I pulled on my magic in such a dramatic fashion.

The cacophony never came though, and instead, only the soft breaths of a sleeping family met my ears.

Curiously, I opened my eyes, letting them adjust for a moment as I oriented myself to the dim tent, a smoldering brasier in the center offering a warm glow that allowed me to just make out colorless shapes. Off to one side was a large sleeping mat, occupied by two bodies, one large and one small—Lord Avis and his wife.

I turned and padded silently around to the other side of the brasier, heading toward a lumpy pile of rugs and cushions. The light, fluttery breaths coming from that corner indicated the nest of pillows served as the Lord's daughter's sleeping place.

When Lord Deryn had given my mission, I had only thought about it in the most abstract of concepts—steal the girl, ransom her back, and claim glory for the Lord who had seen potential in my power.

As the moonlight seeping in through the gaps in the tent flap gleamed across a splash of silver hair, the reality of my task hit me with the force of a stampeding horse. Lord Avis's daughter was beautiful in a way I'd rarely encountered among the barren landscapes of the desert—the bloom of a larrea flower that had forced its way upward through dry, cracked earth.

Long silvery lashes brushed her high cheekbones, nearly translucent as they matched her silvery-white hair—a color I had never seen on another in the Ballan Desert. She lay with her cheek pillowed on a hand, her expression soft, as if she dreamed of something pleasant.

I swallowed thickly as I stepped closer, dropping to my knees before her. Carefully, I passed my hand over her forehead, not quite touching her, but sending a trickle of magic into her mind to persuade her to stay asleep. I had the strange and fleeting hope that it wouldn't disturb whatever dream she had been enjoying.

Before her parents could wake and discover me, I slid my arms beneath her, lifting her easily from the nest of blankets. She murmured in her sleep, and her head turned, falling sideways until her face pressed into the side of my neck. Her body was remarkably soft and warm in my arms, and I swallowed thickly again.

I had broken bones and torn flesh for Lord Deryn. Pulled lightning from a cloudless sky and water from dry earth. But this task—keeping my wits with this beautiful woman so close—would pose a challenge unlike any I had faced for my clan.

CHAPTER TWO

ALYX

I woke to the unmistakable movement of a horse beneath me, but the feeling of incomparable freedom that normally accompanied riding was notably absent. Instead, I was trapped. Arms wrapped around me, one across my chest and one around my waist, keeping me pressed against a firm object at my back: A strong torso.

The second sensation that overwhelmed me was a decidedly masculine scent—the smokiness of campfires and the spice of strong *laka*.

My eyes snapped open to the cloudless sky. It was the stained purple of dawn. My neck ached—my head had lolled back and was supported by a leather-clad shoulder, instead of the softness of the silken pillow in my normal sleeping nest.

I tensed and the arms around me tightened.

"You're safe," a voice murmured near my ear.

Paradoxically, the assurance only stoked the vague sense of unease in my belly into panic. I wrenched my head forward, beginning to squirm. I tried to pull my arms free of the stranger's grasp, but he held me so tightly, I might have been wrestling against steel.

The mount beneath me whickered and a bolt of foreign unease cut through my own panic—the horse's discomfort a clear pang in my power. Against my better judgment, I lessened my struggles. I could never bear the distress of horses, as I felt the bright flame of the desert's magic so clearly in them.

"Where am I?" I demanded instead.

"It's hard to say," the man's voice came again, tone remarkably light despite the depth of his voice that I could feel rumbling in his chest, pressed flush against my back. "Somewhere between Clan Padra and Clan Katal's encampment."

"My parents—"

"Are several hours ride behind us," he cut in. "And the desert is unlikely to help them find their way to us."

His confidence in the desert's favor almost made me scoff, but the way he said it didn't sound like a boast. Just a fact. The panic that I had calmed on the horse's behalf began to rise again, bubbling into my throat where it made my voice rise in pitch.

"Yet you have the gall to insist I'm safe?"

I tried to turn my head to see my captor, but held this close to him, I only managed to give myself a cramp in my already stiff neck. The man's dark hair fluttered at the edge of my vision, as I looked out toward the horizon. Rippling sand dunes glowed golden in the early morning light, spreading out endlessly toward the horizon.

The encampment in which I had fallen asleep and the palms of the oasis were nowhere in sight.

"You have nothing to fear from me," my captor insisted. His casual tone had disappeared, his voice now low and serious. It was such a strange promise from a kidnapper that I was almost tempted to believe him.

My father's voice scolded me in my head, telling me that I was too trusting—too soft for the harsh ways of the desert clans.

"You seriously think you can get away with kidnapping me?" I demanded.

"I believe I already have." My captor's light tone returned.

"Did you..." I swallowed thickly. "Did you hurt my family?"

I had no idea how I could have slept through the fight that must have ensued to get me away. Perhaps I had been drugged? How, I did not know.

"No," he assured. "I had no need to harm anyone."

"Then how..." I frowned.

"The desert willed it so."

My brow only furrowed further. Once again, he seemed assured in the desert's favor—that she would aid him in my kidnapping. Unease crawled up my spine, making me stiffen as if to pull away from him, but his hold made it impossible. The desert's touch had always been strong in me as well, giving me a way with horses and with healing. But it had not been enough to protect me from this strange man.

"Who are you?" I asked.

"I am Kelvar. Warlord of Clan Katal," he proclaimed.

My eyes widened, and once again I tried twisting to see him to no avail. His mount stamped and snorted at my movements, but this time, it was not enough to quell my struggles. Tales of Clan Katal's Warlord had spread across the Ballan Desert like fire through brush. Stories of the storms he could summon and the immense power that let him wield fire like a sword—not that he needed to. His skill with a saber was said to be nearly unmatched as well. Only the strongest Lords could stand against him in a duel.

The last time we crossed paths with Clan Noc, my father and the other Clan Lord had bent together, worrying in hushed whispers about the growing power of Clan Katal, borne by the strength of their Warlord.

"I see my reputation precedes me," he said, seemingly unperturbed as I nearly unseated both of us in my efforts to turn around. "I had hoped to let you ride properly, but if you are going to insist on continuing to upset Dileas, I'll be forced to tie your hands and throw you over her haunches with my bundles."

I stopped squirming. "Dileas... is that your mount?"

"The finest horse in the Ballan Desert," he confirmed.

I pursed my lips, tempted to argue that title belonged to my own stallion, likely now miles behind us in Clan Padra's enclosures. Instead, I said, "A loyal mount to earn such a noble name."

Carefully, I let a small tendril of the desert's magic that grew gently in my mind unfurl, reaching into the consciousness of the horse beneath me. Instantly the mare calmed, and she shook her head and flicked her ears back at me as if to say hello.

I almost smiled despite the direness of my situation. I let my power stroke her mind reassuringly as her gait evened out, only to jolt as I encountered another lick of magic. This power was not the friendly warmth of horses I was used to. It was potent and intoxicating—the crackle of lightning and the siren call of the endless horizon. I could almost smell the metallic warmth that always accompanied magic as I mentally approached.

I reached out to touch it too, utterly unthinking but called in by the inexorable power.

Kelvar flinched behind me, and my magic snapped back into my skull of its own accord.

"Sands," he swore, sitting back and bringing his horse to a halt.

Before I could register what had happened, his hold disappeared from around me, and his solid warmth at my back was gone. A moment later, he stood on the ground at my side, and I got my first good look at Kelvar, Warlord of Clan Katal.

The dark hair I had caught a glimpse of earlier was pulled up into a knot at the back of his head, although part of it still spilled down his neck, and tendrils fell forward to frame his face. His features were proud, his jaw strong. He was much younger than I'd expected for someone of his reputation, but what struck me the most were his dark eyes, currently wide with surprise.

I stared into them, dumbstruck for a long moment. Then, he broke eye contact, shaking himself, as if he had been doused in cold water.

"Do you make a habit of reaching into other people's minds uninvited?" he demanded. Up until this point, his voice had been light. I would have almost called it friendly, if it weren't for the fact he had kidnapped me. Now it was rough but not quite angry.

My shoulders tensed as I shrank back, realizing what I had done. I should have known his power, great as it was rumored to be, would have been intertwined in his own mount's mind. I had unwittingly run my mental fingers over his own consciousness in my quest to befriend his horse.

"It was an accident," I insisted. It did not seem wise to anger my kidnapper, but I had been reckless.

"That was a lot of the desert's magic in my mind for an *accident*," he pointed out.

I swallowed thickly. "I'm sorry." My voice was thin.

I should have known better than to reach out so carelessly. My father always warned me against the dangers of my power—of the untamed desert. It made him protective and fearful in equal measures.

Kelvar blinked, and then his shoulders relaxed from their tense posture, although I sensed it took him great concentration. The stricken expression he wore melted into a confident smirk, seeming both practiced and charming.

"It's fine," he conceded. "Given that I'm the one who kidnapped you, it feels odd for you to be apologizing to me. You know, I don't even know your name."

"Alyx," I offered, glad I had not overly angered my captor in my indiscretion.

"Well, Alyx"—he said my name gently—"it's time I let Dileas rest anyway."

He reached up toward me as if to help me down from his mare's back, but I ignored the outstretched hand. Instead, I swung my leg over and jumped down unaided, landing lightly on my feet before him.

He blinked as I stared up at him, finding him almost an entire head taller than me now that we stood face-to-face. Then he shrugged and walked around to stand at Dileas's head, patting her nose and murmuring to her in a low tone I could not discern. The mare responded by bumping her head into his torso affectionately.

I took advantage of the first reprieve I'd had from my captor since my uncomfortable awakening, looking around. Endless golden sand stretched in every direction, offering no sign of where we had come from or where we were going. Even if I managed to escape from my kidnapper, I would not make it far on foot without any supplies. Kelvar likely knew it as well if he was willing to let me stand here, unbound and unguarded.

I chewed my lips, finding them already dry and chapped, not an uncommon plight in the dry heat of the desert. Kelvar had not been openly hostile to me. In fact, he had been strangely kind, apart from when I had unknowingly shoved my magical fingers into his own power. But my parents' worried faces hovered in my mind.

They had always warned me that the desert's power, burning so brightly in me, would make me a target. I did not know what the Warlord planned for me, but I doubted it would be good.

I glanced down at myself and winced, finding I still wore the thin shift I had gone to sleep in and nothing more. I didn't even have shoes on, and my bare toes dug into the sand, already hot underfoot in the morning sun. There was nothing on my person I could use to my advantage.

Then, a faint glitter at the edge of my vision caught my attention. I looked up to find several packs roped to Dileas's back, and sticking out of one of them, the glimmering handle of a dirk.

I chanced a glance toward the horse's head, where Kelvar had now opened a water sack and was letting Dileas drink. She slurped loudly, covering any noise my movements might make. Before I could second guess myself, I grabbed the handle of the knife and yanked it from the pack. I hid it behind my back, having nowhere on my person to stow it. No matter. I did not plan on concealing it long.

After long moments, Dileas finished drinking, and Kelvar moved to tie the water sack to her back once more. Then, he stepped toward me, a hand reaching to the water skin at his own belt.

"Are you—"

I didn't let him finish the sentence, whipping the dirk out from behind my back and pressing the tip to his throat.

He stilled, and his eyes flashed, but then his confident smile returned, one eyebrow raised.

"Yes?" he asked, as if I had simply called his name to catch his attention.

"Bring me back to Clan Padra," I demanded.

"And why would I do that?"

I looked pointedly at the knife in my hand, its tip currently resting on his Adam's apple. He went nearly cross-eyed looking down at it at this proximity.

"That's a horrible grip, Flower," he mused. "One would think you had never wielded a knife before."

My lips twisted in a grimace, both at the endearment he used so casually and his observation.

Before I could respond, he moved lightning-fast, ducking under the blade in my hand while grabbing my wrist. He twisted, and I yelped as the knife dropped from my hold. He plucked it out of the air deftly.

Then he held it up before me. "Don't tuck your thumb under your other fingers," he explained, showing me the proper grip. "And with your smaller size and inexperience, you'll have better luck taking people by surprise. Stab them in the back, between their fourth and fifth ribs if you can manage it. Or go for their eyes and groin."

I pulled back, looking at him quizzically. "And why are you telling me how to properly hold the knife I just used to threaten you?"

He shrugged. "Maybe so next time you do it, you will be a tad more... well... *threatening*."

I huffed and spluttered in indignation, but he ignored me, only moving to tuck the dirk back into the pack I had pilfered it from. Then, he rifled inside and emerged with a length of rope.

"Unfortunately," he continued, "as ill-conceived as your escape attempt was, it does officially take any chance of leaving you unbound to ride on your own off the table."

I eyed the rope in his hands distastefully, and his responding smile was equal parts rueful and mischievous.

CHAPTER THREE

KELVAR

If carrying a sleeping Alyx had caused me to worry about the success of my mission, then the task of holding an awake Alyx had me teetering on the edge of failure.

I did not worry about her overpowering me and escaping through strength. In fact, I found the unsure way she held a knife downright bizarre for one who had spent their life riding alongside the Lord of a Clan.

I didn't have the mental fortitude to consider such things right now, though. Not when she currently sat before me on Dileas's back, my thighs bracketing hers and one arm around her waist holding her in place as she rested her bound wrists before her.

Every slight breeze caused her silken silver hair to flutter across my face, and I found that it smelled of the larrea flowers I had compared her to when I first saw her. The thought of the blooms made me grimace, and I was glad Alyx couldn't see my face as I screwed my eyes shut in frustration.

I hadn't meant to call her "Flower" earlier, but it had slipped out unbidden.

In fact, I hadn't meant for a lot of things to happen on our journey together, short as it had been so far. I had meant to be detached and aloof, keeping my distance and simply delivering her to Lord Deryn, who would ransom her back to her father in trade for the legendary weaponsmith who rode with Clan Padra. But the moment she woke and stiffened in my arms, I sensed her fear like bitterness on my tongue. And so, I had reassured her she was safe. From there, our interactions only continued to spin out of my control, like an untamed colt barreling ahead despite my desperate pleas for it to stop.

Then, in the moment when her magic brushed against mine, I had nearly flown apart into a million pieces. Lightning had danced at the edge of my consciousness, and my vision went a blinding white. But it was not unpleasant, like losing control so often was. Far from it.

In fact, I almost wished it had been unpleasant.

Now, I glared at the back of the silver head in front of me, trying to puzzle out its contents. I dared not reach out toward her power and risk a repeat of earlier, but curiosity gnawed at me all the same. I sensed licks of magic in many who rode among the clans but nothing like Alyx's.

Hers seemed almost...

Even in my own head I hesitated to continue.

Like *mine*, I forced myself to think. At least in magnitude, if not in quality. If my power was the searing, unforgiving intensity of the desert sun, then hers was the calm majesty of the velvety night sky, lit with endless stars on a moonless night.

Now, Alyx shifted against me, and I gritted my teeth as it pushed her hips back against mine. I wasn't sure which tortured me more, her physical proximity, or the strange ache where my magic lived in the pit of my belly that begged me to reach out and drown in her power once more.

I had to bite my tongue to keep from groaning aloud. I could *not* be having such thoughts. She was a hostage, and after her father agreed to Lord Deryn's price, I would likely never see her again.

Still, I needed a reprieve.

I looked toward the horizon, and my heart sank.

The sun was beginning to set, painting the sky in brilliant oranges and purples as it dipped below the horizon. The dark smudges of tents and an encampment in the distance were nowhere to be found.

I had hoped the desert, in her ever-shifting landscapes, would grant me a short ride back to my own clan. But it was not her will.

With a sigh, I pulled Dileas to a halt.

"We should make camp for the evening."

Alyx huffed. "*We* won't be doing anything unless you untie me." She lifted her bound wrists in illustration.

"*I* will set up camp, while you sit and watch," I clarified with a grimace. Then I slid down off Dileas's back. Before Alyx could attempt to follow, slowed by her immobilized hands, I reached up and lifted her down, slinging her over my shoulder instead of setting her on the ground. She squeaked indignantly and kicked her legs.

"I can walk!" she insisted.

I used one arm banded over her thighs to stop her flailing, instantly becoming aware that she still only wore the thin shift she had been wearing when I took her. The hem was riding dangerously high as she draped over my shoulder.

I swallowed down the thought that I seemed cursed to continue making bad decisions when it came to my charge and used my free hand to rifle around in my packs for another length of rope.

"I know you can," I responded as I carried her over to a pile of boulders near where we had halted. "And if I don't do something about that, you might steal my horse and ride away while I set up our fire."

Bending down, I set her on the ground, so her back was propped against the rocks, and found her scowling at me. "I would never steal a horse."

I raised a brow at her, and she continued to stare me down unwaveringly. I found that I believed her.

Horse theft was one of the highest crimes in the clans, second only to murder. But clansmen were generally not opposed to spilling blood, and I had kidnapped her. Somehow, though, I sensed that she wasn't lying, despite the fact that stealing Dileas might be excusable in these circumstances.

Maybe it was the openness in her gaze, despite her glower. Or perhaps it was the sense of pure brightness that had shot through me when I brushed against her magic earlier.

Still, I shrugged and grabbed her ankles. Even as she kicked against me, I was able to capture them both in one hand. "Maybe you wouldn't, but you already pulled a knife on me once. I would prefer not waking up to my throat slit."

She stopped struggling, likely realizing it was futile, and let me tie her ankles. I could feel her scowling at me as I finished. The weight of her gaze didn't abate as I went about setting up a small camp and building a fire.

CHAPTER FOUR

ALYX

I tensed as I tried and failed to suppress another shiver. As hot as the desert was during the day, it grew brutally cold when the sun went down during the rainy season. The fire Kelvar had built chased away the worst of the chill, but it still seeped through the thin shift I wore and into my bones.

Kelvar had pointedly ignored me since we stopped for the day, but now his gaze darted to where I sat. His hands paused in their motions, brushing through Dileas's mane. He had been tending to her for long minutes, and while I was sure not a single tangle or speck of dust remained in her luxurious mane and tail by now, I could not blame him for indulging. She was a magnificent horse and seemed to enjoy the attention.

It made me miss my own stallion.

I shivered again, and Kelvar put down the brush.

As he rounded the fire and approached me, I eyed him warily. I squeaked in surprise as he scooped me up in his arms.

"What are you doing?" I gasped as he carried me around to the fire, toward Dileas and his own laid-out sleeping mat.

"You're cold," he stated, as if that should make his actions discernable.

I continued to stare at him.

"Dileas and I are warm," he explained.

My heart leaped into my throat as I grasped what he was implying. "You could just give me a robe or something," I pointed out.

"I don't have an extra," he explained as he set me down on his own sleeping mat. "So, we will have to share."

I balked, but I couldn't help but snipe at him, "You captured me in the middle of the night and didn't think about bringing any extra clothes for me?"

"I didn't think about a lot of things when I agreed to this," he murmured, half under his breath, giving me the impression that it was more to himself than it was to me. Then, he clicked his tongue and Dileas obediently picked her way over, before laying down on the far side of the mat from the fire.

The pleasant warm smell of happy horses filled my nose, and already my shivers calmed in their intensity. Kelvar sat down on the opposite side of me, so close his shoulder brushed mine. It shouldn't have been shocking after a day pressed against him on a horse, but I still jumped, a jolt running up my spine.

"Lay down," he instructed.

"Why?"

"Do you normally sleep sitting up?"

I wrinkled my nose but did as he asked, holding my bound wrists close to my chest. Even though I had suspected it was coming, my breath still stuttered as he lay down beside me. He reached out, opening the robe he wore and bundling me into his chest, wrapping the loose fabric around me.

Like this, I thought I might drown in the smoky, spicy scent of him that had danced at the edge of my awareness as we rode. On Dileas's back, with the desert breeze in my face, it hadn't been nearly so potent, but now I realized...

It smelled the same way his magic had felt when I touched it. Like fire and earth and heady *laka*.

My magic grew like a flower, a new leaf unfurling as if to reach out and touch that storm again, but I snapped it back into my head with all the force I could muster.

"Hopefully you can get some sleep. We might have another long day of riding ahead," Kelvar said, his chest rumbling so close to my face that I could feel the vibrations.

"It's not the most comfortable of situations," I snapped, "but I'll manage."

"I'm sorry it's not the pile of fine silks you're used to in Lord Avis's tent, Flower," he retorted, the endearment sounding a bit more derisive than it had the first time he used it. "Not all of us need such luxury. The open sky and stars are enough company for me."

I craned my neck to look up at him, finding him looking pointedly away from me and staring up at the velvet sky. It was indeed beautiful, stars shimmering like gemstones set in a backdrop so dark and rich, I thought I might be able to reach out and touch it.

"I've never slept outside," I admitted.

Kelvar jumped, as if honestly surprised by the simple words. "I thought everybody in the Ballan Desert would have plenty of experience camping under the open sky."

Neither of us looked at each other, both staring up at the darkness of the night. The strange intimacy of his physical proximity, combined with the anonymity of the lack of eye contact, pulled words out of me that I hadn't planned on speaking.

"My parents—my father really—never wanted me to stray too far from his side. He always insisted that my magic would make me a target, even though my power never seemed to grant me the ability to protect myself. I was too soft to be on my own. He was sure something bad would happen to me."

"Sounds rather stupid," Kelvar said, tone flat.

I snorted. "Bold judgement, considering you are the reason I *did* end up getting kidnapped."

A rumble ran through Kelvar's form, and warmth that had nothing to do with his body heat skittered across my skin at the husky sound of his laugh.

"It's not like keeping you near protected you when it came down to it," he pointed out.

I hummed noncommittally. In truth, as I grew older, now a woman and no longer just a girl, my father's protectiveness had begun to chafe—to feel more like captivity than love. It rankled to know that he had been right to fear for me.

Even when I was the one holding a weapon, I posed no threat to true warriors of the Ballan Desert.

But I *hadn't* been hurt, a small voice in the back of my head chimed in. As of yet, nothing more severe than a light chill and an uncomfortable ride had befallen me. Perhaps the world was not so evil as my father feared. Or at least, it didn't have to be.

"I didn't sleep in a tent at all until I was fourteen," Kelvar admitted, drawing me from my reverie with a start.

"Your family didn't prefer having shelter?" I asked, furrowing my brow.

He huffed. "I have no idea what my family might have preferred. My parents were killed by red wolves when I was small."

My heart sank.

"I didn't get a dwelling of my own until Lord Deryn saw potential in the power that had kept me alive on my own for so long and recruited me to start training with the clan riders."

"And now you are a Warlord," I observed. "You went from no tent to the second grandest in the entire clan."

Kelvar shook his head. Some of his hair had come loose of the knot he wore, brushing across my face where I lay with my cheek all but pressed to his solid chest. It was surprisingly soft and ticklish.

"I still live in the small tent I was first given when I became a rider."

"Why?" I asked.

Kelvar's arms flexed around me as he shrugged. "I worked my way up from orphan to Warlord. I have the finest horse and the sharpest sword in the desert. It seems like testing fate to ask for any more of the desert's gifts. Perhaps she has always been pleased with me, because I have not asked her for much."

Something about the statement caused sadness to bloom in my chest. I opened my mouth to point out that he would likely have to find a bigger dwelling when he took a wife and had a family of his own. I snapped my mouth closed with an audible click before I could speak.

We lapsed into silence.

I should have been tense and restless, wrapped in the arms of an enemy Warlord who had stolen me from my bed. But the day had been long, and my vigilance could not last forever. Instead, the warmth of Kelvar at my front and Dileas at my back soaked into my muscles, turning soft and pliant after sitting stiffly on a horse all day.

My mind turned hazy. I thought I heard Kelvar murmur, "Sleep well, Flower," as I drifted off, but it might have been part of my dreams.

CHAPTER FIVE

KELVAR

Dileas stared at me accusingly over Alyx's sleeping form. I glared back at her, and she flicked a judgmental ear.

I tried to silently argue with her—and myself—that this was simply more efficient than giving Alyx my robe and then trying to huddle against Dileas for warmth. Then we both would have to spend the night sleepless and cold.

As it was, it seemed that I would still be spending tonight awake and uncomfortable. Alyx's soft form pressed against me as her light, sleepy breaths tickled my throat was torture.

Many women I had briefly shared a tent with had fallen asleep as I held them, and it had always been pleasant. But never had I had such a visceral urge to bury my face in their hair and inhale. Or to hold them so tightly that the magic that spilled off their skin in calming, effervescent waves might permeate the storm that constantly danced and sparked in my own flesh.

And never had it been a worse idea to do these things.

Dileas snorted, as if reminding me that I had also let my casual endearment slip again.

Flower.

I wrinkled my nose, trying to discern how this mission had gone so far off the path in just one day.

Still, it was not unsalvageable. It had only taken me a day to ride from Clan Katal to Clan Padra. If the desert was not angry, and I had no reason to believe she would be, it shouldn't take me any longer to get back.

Half a day's ride and I could have enough space from Alyx to think clearly—to realize how catastrophically stupid it was to be having these feelings. The desert had already blessed me an inordinate amount to allow me to rise from an orphan hunting for myself with nothing more than a pilfered sling and stones to the most feared Warlord in the desert. I would not throw it all away by risking the ire of not one, but two Clan Lords, all because I couldn't ignore the way Alyx's hair smelled like larrea flowers. Or the way the calming waves of her magic felt like the ocean caressing the sands—at least the way I always imagined it in the legends, for I had never crossed the desert to see it.

I groaned quietly and laid my head down on my mat, resisting the visceral urge to tuck Alyx's head under my chin.

One more day, and I could be free of this torment.

As the sun dipped rapidly toward the horizon on our second day of riding, I bit back a sigh of annoyance. Alyx shifted before me, clearly uncomfortable after a full day of riding without rest as well. I had driven us hard, hoping the tents of Clan Katal's encampment would appear on the horizon if we just covered enough ground, but to no avail.

The Ballan desert was prone to shifting based on her mood. Journeys that took a day when she was pleased could take two weeks when she was in a rage. All who rode the sands knew to both respect and fear our home, knowing our very survival depended on her goodwill—the goodwill that had been earned when the first man crossed from the mountains to the ocean and tamed the monster-infested wilderness of the burning sands.

While I enjoyed riding through the wilds, rarely were my journeys long when time was of the essence. Today, though, the desert sought to vex me.

We would not be making it to Clan Katal before the sun set, and I would be faced with another sleepless night, either letting Alyx share my warmth or leaving her to freeze in the elements.

I already knew which option I would pick, as torturous as it would be.

With a sigh, I shifted my weight back on my sit bones, and Dileas ambled to a stop beside a cliff-like formation of weathered rocks.

"We will camp here for the night," I declared, before dismounting.

Alyx, unable to support her weight with her hands bound, slid down with more force than she otherwise might have from Dileas's considerable height.

Unconsciously, I reached out to catch her. My hands grasped her waist, pulling her close to me and setting her gently on her feet. Despite having her pressed to me all day, I was jarred by her sudden closeness—the slight catch of her breath and the way she leaned back into me for just a moment as she gained her balance.

Hastily, she stepped away, and I snatched my hands back, rubbing them on my robe to dispel the warmth of her skin that had bled through the thin shift she still wore.

Not for the first time, I cursed myself for not thinking to bring more clothing.

I stepped around her to unload a few packs from Dileas's back.

"After I start a fire, I'm going to have to go hunting," I explained. "I didn't bring enough meat for more than one person for more than one night."

Alyx huffed. "That was poor planning. It seems that Lord Deryn doesn't keep you around for your brains."

I snorted. "Thankfully, my skill with a saber is more than enough to recommend me."

Alyx didn't answer, instead bending from side to side to relieve some of the stiffness that accumulated in one's spine after a day on horseback. I looked away quickly as it caused the hem of her shift to ride up, showing a dangerous amount of toned thigh.

Instead, I busied myself with building the fire in the protection offered by the rocky formation I had chosen as our campsite. After making a pile of brush supplied by the obliging dry scrub in the area, I waved my hand over it. With a lick of power unleashed in its direction, it burst into flame, although with slightly more force than I had intended.

"Sands," I cursed under my breath as it immediately consumed half of the kindling I had carefully arranged.

Alyx looked curiously in my direction, and I shook myself.

"Sit down," I instructed, inclining my head at the space before the fire.

She made a face but did as I asked, while I fetched the length of rope from my packs. While I couldn't have her ankles bound while we rode, it wouldn't do to have her running off while I hunted.

When I approached her with the rope, Alyx glared at me.

"Where would I possibly go?" she asked.

"I don't want to find out," I countered. "Besides, if you have nowhere to run, then why would you object to me stopping you from fleeing?"

I kneeled before her and held out a hand expectantly. Alyx's nostrils flared in frustration, and she lifted her foot, managing to kick a healthy amount of sand in my face as she did so.

As I spat it from my mouth and blinked it from my eyes, the look of satisfaction on her face indicated it had been intentional. I worked quickly to tie her ankles together, focusing on the grit now stuck in my teeth and stinging my eyes. It was a good reminder that she remained my prisoner—and strictly off limits—despite the way my thumb unconsciously soothed over the arch of her foot as I finished off the knot.

I stood, dusting off my hands, and tried not to think about the way Alyx looked, sitting in the sand and staring daggers at me with her hands and feet bound. Quickly, I grabbed my saber and slung it over my back.

"I'll be back," I said, stalking off into the open sands.

The open air and the thrill of the hunt would do my churning mind good after a day sharing a horse with Alyx, before a night of her bundled in my arms.

CHAPTER SIX

ALYX

I stared into the fire, its merry crackling at odds with my bubbling frustration.

Every second I waited without making another escape attempt, the louder my father's voice echoed in my mind, telling me I needed to be protected.

Even as we rode, my hands bound, toward an enemy encampment, I didn't feel unsafe with Kelvar. A fact that only prompted my father's voice to argue that I was being incredibly naïve. The Warlord had stolen me from my bed in my sleep and absconded with me across the sands.

Still, after two days in his presence, I felt assured that if he were going to hurt me, he would have done so by now. Not to mention, his quiet admissions as he held me next to the fire last night had seemed far too vulnerable for one with nefarious intentions.

No—Kelvar would not hurt me.

As we rode in oddly companionable silence, the thought that had grown like a pebble in my boot from a small irritation to a festering wound, was the thought of what would happen *after* Clan Katal ransomed me back to my father. The small amount of freedom I had been afforded, from the occasional ride alone to the time I spent healing injured riders, would disappear. The argument that I should be able to sleep on my own and spend my time with whom I chose would be snuffed out. I had been kidnapped once, and clearly I must be guarded even closer to keep it from happening again.

But if I escaped from Kelvar and returned to Clan Padra, such arguments would be dashed. I would have proven that I could protect myself.

Such thinking didn't change the fact that I was indeed safer with Kelvar than I would be wandering the desert alone without a horse or protection, though.

I narrowed my eyes at the campfire, as if it might hold answers, but that too only frustrated me. It had sprung to life with nearly explosive energy as Kelvar held out his hand. While I had been gifted with immense power—healing and calming horses and even calling plants to life in impossibly dry soil—such things had always been beyond me. Perhaps if they had not, I wouldn't be in such a position.

I ripped my eyes from the dancing flames to instead look out at the horizon. I could no longer see Kelvar in the deepening twilight.

Instead, I admired the ombre sky, staining from fiery orange to dusty purple as the sun disappeared below the tops of the dunes.

A puff of dust appeared in the distance, and I squinted. Perhaps Kelvar had found prey and was giving chase. The cloud grew closer, and I frowned. It seemed far too large to be produced by Kelvar on foot, and he had left Dileas behind. In fact, it seemed large enough to indicate the pounding hooves of several mounts.

I struggled to my feet, a difficult task with my wrists and ankles bound together, but I managed. With a better view, I could see that indeed a group of three riders galloped in our general direction. At this distance, I could not make out the color of their clan sashes.

Still, an ember of hope lit in my chest. I could not make it back to my clan alone, but perhaps I could convince these riders to bring me back. My father would surely reward them for returning me unharmed—a price that would still be less than whatever the Lord of Clan Katal demanded. Or even better, I could offer my healing skills to their clan in exchange for aid in returning to my family.

I raised my bound wrists in the air, desperately waving to make myself visible. I even jumped up and down, stumbling a bit with the constraints of doing so while bound, but I did not relent.

The riders drew closer, but they appeared to only be riding in the general direction of the rocky cliff we camped against.

"Over here! Help!" I shouted.

The riders swerved, barreling straight toward our camp. My heart leaped into my throat with both nerves and relief. I did not know these riders, but this would be my chance to prove to my parents that I was not so helpless as they supposed.

As they drew closer, I squared my shoulders and raised my chin.

I was a daughter of the Ballan Desert, and I would act as such.

Dust whirled around me as the group of three riders encircled me, and I fought to not cough around it as I blinked against the burning in my eyes.

"What is a little thing like you doing alone in the desert?" the leader of the group asked before I could clear my throat and speak.

His tone instantly made me bristle, but I tried to stand my ground. His sash was the blue of Clan Tibel, and the snarling hyena of the clan's emblem adorned the handle of the dirk at his waist. My father was not enemies with the Lord of Clan Tibel, but neither were they friends.

"I could use your aid," I admitted. "I've been captured from my clan, and I need help to return."

"Why not just take his horse and run?" another of the men asked, jerking his chin toward Dileas.

Dread settled like a rock in my belly. No good men would suggest such a thing. Horses were sacred to the desert, as was the bond between horse and rider. I would not steal Dileas, who stood near the fire watching us warily.

"I am the daughter of the Lord of Clan Padra, and I have more honor than a common horse thief." I raised my chin as I spoke.

"If you still have honor, this hasn't been a proper kidnapping," the first man snorted, and the other two chuckled darkly in response.

Nausea bubbled up in my throat. Even waking up on a foreign horse, held to Kelvar's chest after being whisked away in my sleep, I hadn't felt as unsafe as I did surrounded by these riders. I made to step back, forgetting my feet were bound and tripping.

Before I could fall, the third man reached down and grabbed me by the arm. My shoulder wrenched painfully as I lost my footing, and I tried to pull out of his grasp. His fingers only dug deeper into my flesh, and I squeaked in pain.

"Whoever kidnapped you didn't do a very good job, tying you up nicely and leaving you for us to find," he commented.

I grasped on to the threads of my original plan, even as they slipped through my fingers. "I'm a healer," I insisted. "If you bring me to your clan's encampment, surely there are some people there I can help."

"Oh, we will take you back to our Clan Lord," the one holding me promised. "He'll decide on the best use for your talents."

I tried to pull my arm out of his hold again to no avail. "If this is how your Clan Lord allows his riders to behave, then Clan Tibel does not deserve the desert's favor."

I finally succeeded in wrenching my arm from the man's hold, only for my struggling to overbalance me. I tripped over the rope around my ankles and stumbled into another's horse. I slammed into the solid wall of muscle that was the animal's flank, dazed enough that I didn't notice the third rider had stepped up behind me, boxing me in

He leaned down from his horse, grabbing me by the hair hard enough to make my eyes water. My shriek of pain was cut off by his hand clamping over my mouth.

"If you are going to insult us, maybe we won't bring you back to our Lord at all," he sneered in my ear.

A displeased whinny sounded from by the fire, Dileas clearly unhappy with my distress.

"Let's get her out of here before whoever left her comes back," the leader of the trio instructed.

As the man holding me dragged me backward, my heart fluttered against my rib cage in fear and even more potent... *anger*. My eyes burned and a trapped scream filled my throat. My efforts to prove that I could take care of myself had backfired in the worst possible way. These horrid men were proving my father right, and the thought made fury flare within me. I kicked and struggled, my vision blurring with unshed tears, as the man seated on the horse before me laughed at my antics.

The laugh cut off in a horrible gurgle. Crimson splattered over his horse's neck, and I blinked the wetness from my eyes in surprise. A wicked slash cut across his throat. His eyes were wide with shock, even as blood bubbled from his lips.

His mount screamed in panic, rearing and bucking. The rider, already a corpse, slipped from his back and fell to the ground with a lifeless thump. Now riderless, the horse bolted, running off into the sands.

"Take your filthy hands off her, or I will cut them off," a voice came from one side. It was familiar, but the icy cold tone was not like anything I had ever heard before.

I turned my head as best as I could while still trapped, my scalp burning with the strain. Kelvar stood with his hand outstretched, sparks dancing around his fingertips. He hadn't even needed a weapon to kill that man—just the magic he wielded was enough.

My captor didn't let go, but he backed his mount up a few steps, dragging me with him, even as a metallic ringing indicating he had drawn his saber. The point came to rest at my collarbone.

The last rider drew his sword too, seemingly the bravest of the lot, as he pointed it at Kelvar. Relief and fear flowed through me in equal measure at his appearance and the promise of violence he brought with him.

Kelvar's gaze was even sharper than the sword he drew from across his own back—a sword with curved quillons and a blade longer than any I had seen before. It might have been almost comically large if not for the deadly confidence with which he held it.

The remaining two horses whickered and pawed the ground nervously as Kelvar faced off against my two captors, and a bolt of their distress penetrated my skull. I blinked.

My magic was not good for destruction but had an affinity for one other thing besides healing—horses. With all three men distracted by their swords, I closed my eyes, gently unfurling a tendril of magic toward each horse's mind.

I ignored the feel of Dileas, still hovering nearby, and instead reached into the consciousness of the two other mounts. I offered a mental apology for what I was about to do. Then, I injected them with a bolt of borrowed fear—the way my heart had hammered when the first man grabbed me and the dread I felt at knowing I wouldn't be able to escape.

The effect was instantaneous. Screams of fright split the air, and the horse at my back began to buck and prance. The hand disappeared from my hair, as the rider was forced to grab on to his mount or risk being thrown from his seat.

The other horse reacted similarly, bolting off into the sands despite his rider's attempts to control him. I stumbled forward, falling to my knees out of the way, as the third rider was carried away by his frightened and uncooperative horse, yelling and swearing in surprise.

As I blinked the dust their sudden flight had kicked up from my eyes, I looked up to see Kelvar, whose expression of stony rage had melted into one of surprised confusion. As our gazes met, though, his expression fell into one of concern.

In one motion, he had sheathed his sword and fallen to his knees before me.

"Are you hurt?" He asked, reaching out toward me, then hesitating. "Did they... did any of them..."

He trailed off, rage beginning to bubble in his eyes as his gaze skated over my ruffled appearance. I shook my head quickly.

"It was just a very unpleasant conversation," I admitted. "When you distracted them, I convinced their mounts that it was time for that conversation to be over."

He blinked at me in surprise, and then a tiny smile toyed at his lips, although his eyes still held the smoldering embers of anger. The expression made something in my chest twitch, not altogether unpleasantly, but I shoved it away.

"And here I thought they fled because I was just that terrifying," he said.

I huffed. "Maybe you only like to think you are so fearsome."

Even as I said it though, my gaze was drawn to the slumped corpse off to one side, just at the edge of my vision. The hair at the back of my neck stood on end as the horrible gurgle he had made replayed in my mind. Kelvar had killed him with just a wave of his hand—without even drawing his weapon.

The thought should terrify me more. I should be just as scared to be trapped with him as I was to be with the other riders—even more terrified now that I knew the tales of his fearsome power were true.

But I couldn't help the relief I felt as he kneeled before me.

Now, he pulled a small knife from his boot, like one he would use for skinning animals. He reached out, grabbing the rope between my bound wrists before slicing through it with a decisive *snick*.

I looked up at him in surprise and cocked my head.

"I'd rather have you steal my horse and run away than be unable to defend yourself against other riders," he said, tone firm. "Although, after that trick with the horses..." He shrugged as he gestured for me to show him my ankles, so he could cut those ropes too. "Maybe you aren't as defenseless as the way you hold a knife would make it seem."

I wrinkled my nose at him at the reminder of my ineptitude, but my chest still warmed. I had not escaped, but somehow Kelvar seeing more competence in my actions than my father ever did still felt like a victory.

When I was no longer tied, Kelvar stood and reached out a hand to help me to my feet. His fingers were callused and warm against mine, and I didn't let go right away. He didn't move away either. Shocks of adrenaline still ran through me from the encounter, but his touch was comforting in its gentle firmness.

"You're sure you're all right?" he asked, voice low and uncharacteristically serious.

I nodded. "I'm tougher than I look."

"I can tell," he said without a shadow of doubt in his voice. His gaze skated over me, and the warmth of his proximity enveloped me, paradoxically making me shiver in its contrast to the rapidly cooling evening air.

Seeing my shudder, he frowned and looked away.

"At least we gained one thing from this unpleasant encounter," he observed. "We found you a change of clothes."

Chapter Seven

Kelvar

Alyx sat with her knees held close to her chest, eyes closed as she enjoyed the warmth of the fire. The robe she wore now was slightly too big, and the loose pants too long, requiring her to roll them up a few times at the ankles before shoving her feet into too-large boots. At least I had slit the man's throat instead of stabbing him through the chest, and there were only a few errant drops of dried blood near the collar.

I observed her as I turned the strips of meat from the jackrabbit I had caught on their sticks in the fire. As much as I was happy she would be warmer—and I would no longer have to endure the infuriating sight of her in nothing but a thin shift—it irked me to see her in the clothes of the man who had attacked her.

I grit my teeth so hard they creaked in my skull at the memory and tore my gaze away from her, turning it back toward the fire.

The rage that had consumed me when I returned to the camp to find her surrounded by unfamiliar riders had been blinding. At the sight of how she kicked and fought against the man who held her by the hair, I had thrown out my hand without thinking. Magic had shattered out of me, and the first man was dead before I even realized what I was doing.

I frowned at the strips of meat, now sizzling and popping as they finished cooking. I had no right to be so angry at the thought of her being kidnapped—after all, I had captured her first, right out from under her own parents' noses.

Alyx hummed under her breath. "That smells good."

I pulled one stick out of the fire and handed it to her. She smiled at me as she took it. I started to smile back but jerked my gaze away before I could fully commit to the expression.

The urge to care for her was too strong. I had jumped to her protection and itched to feed her and clothe her—this time in *my* clothes. But I couldn't be having these thoughts. I would be delivering her to my Lord, hopefully tomorrow, before these urges took root in my mind and would not let go.

If the desert granted me her favor, I could soon be done with this whole misadventure. It would be for the best.

I did not know what I had done to earn the desert's ire, but I was ready to offer her all the blood I could spare to lose to be forgiven.

We rode for three days and nights with no sign of an encampment on the horizon. Each day, Alyx perched on Dileas's back before me, her back pressed flush to my front. And each night, I watched her sleep by the fire, both relieved and pained that I no longer had to bundle her in my own robe and hold her close for warmth.

Every night, I laid awake for far too long, trying not to think about the way she had felt pressed against the planes of my body as I held her to me—what I would do if she wasn't the daughter of the Lord of a rival clan. Having her near, but just out of reach, began to drive me to distraction.

But it wasn't just her proximity.

It was the way she didn't seem afraid, despite being my captive. It was the way she doted on Dileas, running her finger through her mane as I built our fire every night. My mare seemed to have betrayed me as well, stretching into the touch and whickering happily each time.

On the second day, I brought it up.

"You said you would never steal my horse, but I notice you didn't say anything about turning her against me," I pointed out as Alyx scratched Dileas's withers in a way that made the mare go slack jawed with pleasure. "Is that your newest plan for escape?"

"If she does turn against you for me, it's simply because she has good taste in humans," Alyx commented, seemingly unperturbed.

"Excuse me? What have I done to earn such insults?"

Alyx arched a silvery brow. "Besides kidnapping me in the dead of night and holding me for ransom against my will?"

I grimaced. "Actually, don't answer that. I'd rather not know. I have my charms, though."

"Really?" She cocked her head. "Where have you been hiding them?"

My lips twitched. "I normally don't bring them on kidnapping missions."

Alyx hummed noncommittally and turned her attention back toward the horse. While her father clearly saw the softness in her that endeared her to my mount, he certainly seemed to underestimate her resilience, if her willingness to verbally spar with me was any indication.

I also couldn't ignore the way she soldiered on bravely, without complaint, day after day. After her admission that she had never slept outside, I expected the hard riding and days with nothing to eat but dried jackrabbit meat and dates to grate on her.

Instead, she seemed even more energized as time wore on. She appeared almost excited as she watched the landscapes shift around us from powdery dunes to rocky cliffs to baked earth dotted with hard scrub. I might have expected her brush with the riders of Clan Tibel to make her more skittish, but it was as if the proof that she was not completely helpless had only bolstered her confidence.

It only made her more beautiful.

As I watched her light the fire for us the third night—she had insisted on helping with camp now that I no longer kept her bound—a proud smile grew across her face. I had the sinking feeling that being my captive was the most freedom she had ever been allowed.

So, she bloomed like a flower in the rainy season, and I grew more exhausted and brittle by the hour.

Late afternoon on the third day, a splotch of green in the distance signaled an oasis. I reached forward and pointed so Alyx could see my hand where she sat in front of me.

"We can stop there for the night. It's been too long since we have had shade and fresh water," I observed.

Alyx nodded. "Dileas could use the rest."

She patted the mare's neck, and Dileas tossed her head as if in appreciation at the consideration. I squeezed my thighs around my mount, as if asking whose side she was on. After all, it was not like I hadn't been checking her hooves and grooming her every night. Still, Dileas seemed to have decided Alyx was her preferred human at the moment.

In response, Dileas decided that this was her signal to break into a full gallop. My magical hand on her consciousness knew she could tell that wasn't my intent, but she was willful.

I had always liked that about her.

I threw my arms around Alyx's waist, afraid she might be unseated by the sudden acceleration.

I needn't have bothered. She already leaned over Dileas's neck, moving as one with the mount as if she were born on horseback.

She might not have fought like a clansman of the desert, but she rode like one. Better than most, in fact.

Despite her competence, I could not bring myself to let go of her waist, tucking my chin over her shoulder and holding tight as we hurtled toward the oasis in the distance. Her hair mixed with Dileas's mane, tickling my face and smelling like freedom.

A whoop split the air, and it took me a second to realize that Alyx was laughing at the unrestrained joy of the sudden sprint. I couldn't help the broad smile that split my own face. It wasn't the self-assured smirk I wore so often when doing my Lord's bidding—the one that was more practiced than I let on, crafted to give the impression of power and certainty.

This was a real smile, and a laugh of my own followed hot on its heels.

Too soon, we hurtled past the palm trees at the edge of the oasis, and Dileas slowed to a walk, and then a stop, pawing the ground happily at the edge of a crystalline pool.

I dismounted. Alyx hopped down after me unaided.

I turned to look at her, planning to compliment her riding in the face of Dileas's free spirit.

My voice caught in my throat.

Alyx's cheeks were flushed, and her silvery eyes sparkled with joy. I had the fleeting thought when I first saw her, sleeping in her father's tent illuminated only by a sliver of moonlight, that she was the most beautiful woman I had ever seen. I had quickly shoved that thought aside, chiding myself for thinking such a thing about a woman I was about to hold for ransom.

Now, under the sun with her face split by a broad smile, there was no escaping the truth of the matter. She was the brightness and life and freedom of the desert, all encapsulated in a single person.

I stared at her, dumbstruck, as though seeing her for the first time, despite our close proximity over the last days.

I didn't hear the warning trill until it was too late.

A pained scream filled the air, and Dileas reared in fear, front hooves lashing out. Before her, a family of three caracals hissed and spat, crouched in preparation to pounce. Muscles bunched with lethal strength in their long feline bodies and the black tufts on the tips of their ears quivered. Alyx whirled around, hands outstretched as if she were prepared to try to reason with the predators.

Time slowed, the sound sucking from my mind even as I saw Alyx's mouth open to shout. The magic of the desert flared in my skull, connecting me to every living thing and grain of sand for miles—Alyx a raging bonfire of power so bright, I could barely make out the flickering flames of the caracals beside her.

I leaped into action, jumping between her and the animals and throwing my hands out, unleashing a lick of power at the closest flame of life. One of the caracals flew back, hitting a rock at the edge of the pool with a thud and a whimper.

The others were not deterred. I unsheathed my saber from my back, slicing it downward in a savage slash just as another creature jumped at me, forcing it to retreat out of my blade's reach.

"Run!" I commanded, both shouting with my voice and sending a bolt of intention toward Dileas through our connected minds. As open to the power of the desert as I was during battle, the command came unconsciously.

I barely had time to register retreating hoofbeats and a scrabbling behind me as both Alyx and Dileas hurried to obey before the caracals advanced, two at once this time.

I threw my saber up in time to slash one across the chest, but the third had circled toward my unarmed side. It crashed into me hard enough to rattle my teeth. Together, we tumbled to the ground, a tangled ball of limbs and tearing claws. I managed not to impale myself on my own saber as we rolled, but it fell from my grip as my head connected with the hard earth.

White flared behind my eyes, blinding me momentarily, as a tearing pain seared across my shoulder. Sightlessly, I threw my arms out, wrestling with the writhing, furry creature that pinned me to the ground.

Power flared unbidden, the presence of the desert in my mind turning to an all-consuming shriek. A pulse of magic exploded out of me with a wordless shout. The weight on my chest disappeared and did not return.

I blinked to clear my vision and struggled to sit up. The creature that had pinned me lay on the ground several meters away, smoking gently, a large, charred circle marring the golden fur of its body.

The one I had thrown back originally struggled to its feet and beat a hasty retreat, sensing that it was outmatched. I sighed heavily in relief marred by frustration.

I grit my teeth, ready to berate myself for not being aware of other visitors to the watering hole. Alyx's presence had left me distracted and unbalanced.

Such thoughts flew from my head as another scream filled the air, followed by a flash of pain in my mind.

Dileas.

I flew to my feet, injured shoulder forgotten.

"Kelvar!" Alyx called out, but I was already moving, running and stumbling forward before I had fully stood.

She kneeled on the ground, a short run away from where I had fallen. Dileas lay on her side before her, and my heart dropped.

In seconds, I was at their sides, nearly shoving Alyx out of the way to get to my mount. My heart plummeted from my chest into the baked earth below me.

Dileas's foreleg was bent at an odd angle. Pain and despair rose in my throat, choking me at the sight of bone poking through her silken coat. Blood dripped down her hoof to stain the ground below.

"She panicked and stepped in a fox hole," Alyx said at my side, her voice tremulous, as if with pain. I barely heard it. It sounded as if I were underwater.

I had done this. I hadn't watched for predators, and when I ordered her to run away, I had sent my normally surefooted mount into a frenzy.

My eyes burned, and the hairs on the back of my neck lifted, as sparks began to dance across my skin. Where before, sound had been sucked out of my surroundings as the focus of battle set it, now, it pushed in on me: Dileas's labored breathing and Alyx's voice as she tried to say something I was too overwhelmed to understand.

Thunder rumbled far too close, and I knew it was my doing, but I could do nothing to stop it. I turned my face up to the sky and screamed. The sound was carried away by the howling of wind, as lightning split the sky, and I was lost in a storm of rage and magic.

Chapter Eight

Alyx

I clapped my hands to my ears, trying to block out the noise of howling wind and bone-rattling thunder. It did nothing, though, to drown out the screaming in my head.

It was as if the magic of the desert was being torn apart. The gentle growing force that lived in my mind was nowhere to be found. It had been replaced by a wild, feral thing.

And that wild thing currently kneeled on the ground before me.

Kelvar's face was screwed up in pain as he tilted it toward the sky. But he was not just a man. He was a storm in human skin. Now it had burst out of him in rage and pain in response to Dileas's injury. His fists were clenched on his knees so hard his knuckles turned white, and he was perfectly still outside of a fine tremor that spoke to tension running through every muscle.

The mare beside him thrashed, as if she wanted to flee the chaos of the flashing lighting and torrential winds that whipped her mane. White shone around her eyes as they rolled in both pain and fear.

I could help her, but not like this.

On my hands and knees, I inched forward toward Kelvar. The storm pushed against me as if with physical hands. I bowed my head and persisted, gritting my teeth until I sat just before him.

"Kelvar!" I shouted, but the wind carried my voice away. He did not even twitch in response.

I brought one hand to his shoulder and jolted as a spark shocked my skin. Still, I grabbed it and shook, trying to jostle him from whatever trance he was in.

The howling of the wind quieted infinitesimally, but lightning still crackled and danced around us. His dark hair pulled free of its knot and whipped around his face as he kneeled motionless in the storm. This close to him, I could see the deep furrow between his brows and even the glistening of tears clinging to his lashes. It struck me again just how young he was—not any older than I, saddled with this immense burden.

The rush of magic through his body must be agonizing.

I moved my hand from his shoulder to his cheek, lifting the other to mirror it. I cupped his face as gently as I could, at odds with the chaos around us.

"You're safe." My words could barely be heard over the storm. I didn't know why I echoed his first words to me, but they felt right on my tongue.

"You're safe, and I'm here," I repeated.

The wind whipping my hair slowed. And the next crack of thunder somehow seemed less violent. So, I kept going.

"I'm here, and I'm not going to leave you. I'll help you."

The furrow between Kelvar's smoothed. The wild calmed, turning from a gale into a breeze. I sighed in relief, but I did not let go of his face.

His eyes didn't open yet, but he took a shuddering breath in. "Dileas..."

"I'm going to help her," I promised.

At this, his eyes finally snapped open. His hands shot to my own wrists, pinning them in place where they held his cheeks, not that I had planned to move them yet. I sucked in a breath at the look in his eyes—wet with tears but with nearly glowing with the magic that still clung to him. Vulnerable and lethal at the same time.

"I can't let you... I can't kill her," he admitted.

I shook my head. "I'm not going to. I promise."

His expression was so hopeless, my heart nearly cracked. But with the storm of his magic quieting, the pained fear of the horse behind me began seeping back in. Gently, I extricated myself from Kelvar's grip.

"Just keep Dileas calm," I said, shifting on my knees until I faced the mare once more. "She trusts you."

It was true. The bond between rider and horse was nearly palpable in the magic of the desert, bending the fabric of power with its weight.

"What do you—" Kelvar started, but I was already reaching out to Dileas's injured leg.

My power sprang forth easily, as if it had been called to life as Kelvar's had calmed. Tendrils of life bloomed in my chest and crawled down my hand toward Dileas. I wasn't sure if I closed my eyes or if my vision simply faded as I became one with the network of vitality that spread through the creatures of the desert—and right beneath my fingers, a rent in the tapestry.

As my magic reached out to touch it, Dileas squealed, but Kelvar's voice followed, shushing and soothing nonsensically. I let the noises of the world fade into the background as I focused all my attention on the tear in front of me.

Carefully, I picked at the loose threads, pulling them together and untangling them where they had become knotted. As delicately as possible, I began weaving together what had been torn apart.

I drifted in magic for an indeterminate period of time. It was always like this when I healed—no sense of anything but my own power and the fabric of life that needed mending.

As I settled the last thread into place, and at last the snag disappeared, I finally let myself slip back into my body. My vision blurred, and I blinked previously sightless eyes until they finally focused. My hand lay on Dileas's foreleg, but where there had been protruding bone now only lay a pale, thin scar. The awkward bend of her joint was gone.

"*Sands.*"

Kelvar's swear almost made me jump in surprise, but my muscles only twitched weakly, as if they weren't quite responding to my brain yet. I lifted my head, the world spinning around me as I tried to meet Kelvar's gaze, although my own eyes would barely focus.

He kneeled across from me by Dileas's head.

"I told you I would help," I said, but the words came out slurred, my tongue feeling several sizes too large for my mouth. How long had it been since I had a sip of water?

"You did more than help. You worked miracles," he murmured. The words sounded very far away.

I wanted to say that I could do no such thing, but further speech was beyond me. Instead, I managed a slight twitch of my lips before I began tipping sideways. My muscles were too tired to brace myself for impact with the ground beneath me, but it never came. Instead, strong arms caught me, and a familiar storm enveloped me—but this time, it was not a torrent of destruction and rage. This time, it was the gentle rumble of thunder on the horizon and the comforting thought of desert rain, and I burrowed into a warm chest and fell asleep.

Chapter Nine

Kelvar

I couldn't help but stare, watching Alyx's shoulder rise and fall as she breathed deeply in sleep. It was so slight and delicate, that I couldn't even conceive how such power was packed into such a tiny frame.

Sometimes, my own body felt too small to contain the vastness of the desert that pulsed within me. When I opened myself up to the rush of life and death, the awareness of the landscape around me pounded at the inside of my skull as if trying to break free. But I must weigh twice as much as Alyx, and she seemed to contain the power with ease.

The tales whispered around campfires claimed that I carried the most power ever seen in the desert, and while I had my misgivings, Lord Deryn encouraged this gossip. But now my doubts solidified.

I had thought there must have been another Clan Lord in history who could match me, but I had never expected to find it in such a form.

A snuffle drew my attention, and I tore my gaze from Alyx's sleeping form to check on Dileas. Disbelief still coursed through me as I watched her stand, picking at the tough desert grass that grew in the softer ground around the oasis. She didn't even favor her injured leg. I wouldn't believe it had been broken at all if the image wasn't seared into my memory in horrific detail.

My gaze darted back to Alyx's sleeping form, and my sense of wonder returned, laced with worry. She had slept like the dead since she collapsed at Dileas's side, not stirring at all when I set up camp and moved her close to the fire, even bundling her in my own robe.

I couldn't fathom the toll such healing would have taken on her. In fact, I couldn't fathom how it had been done at all. Fire and lightning and destruction flew to my fingertips without a second thought, but never had I been able to heal even the smallest cut.

As I thought about it, the three long scratches across my shoulder where the caracal's claws had raked me pulsed with pain. Such skills would be useful. Perhaps more useful than the ones I had been given.

I shook myself. The desert had already granted me so much—more than I deserved. I would simply use the powers I had to keep Alyx safe while she slept. I could manage that much at least.

⚬———————⊷⟡⊶·———————⚬

Worry gnawed at my bones like a scavenging hyena as the sun neared its zenith. Alyx still hadn't woken, even when I moved her into the lean-to I had constructed against one of the larger rock formations to protect her from the searing sun.

I wanted to hunt for fresh meat—surely she would be famished when she awoke—but I was wary of leaving her and Dileas unprotected. The memory of the rider of Clan Tibel grabbing her by the hair also jumped to mind, and a lump of molten iron formed in my throat. As we had learned yesterday, many creatures of the desert gathered at water sources, and not all of them took kindly to sharing.

Thinking of water, I furrowed my brow. Alyx hadn't drunk any water in over twelve hours either, a dangerous proposition in the Ballan Desert. While the nights were cold, the days burned hot and dry enough to sap moisture from you fast enough to leave you dizzy on the ground if you didn't pay attention.

Alyx needed to wake, if only to eat and drink something.

I stood from my seat on a flat rock near the edge of the pool, making sure I had my water skin before ducking into the small lean-to. It was low enough that I had to crawl on my hands and knees to reach Alyx.

I hesitated, watching her sleep for just a moment. Her delicate lashes brushed against her high cheekbones, and my heart stuttered. I had known she was beautiful the night I stole her from Clan Padra's encampment, but I hadn't known the strength she held.

I hadn't even considered the way that strength might be a calming presence against my own, drawing me from my storm and soothing me into the gentle patter of desert rain. The stutter in my chest turned into an ache, and I gritted my teeth.

I wasn't supposed to want.

I reached out toward Alyx and brushed my hand over her brow, just like I had the first night I saw her. Although this time, instead of wishing her oblivion, I let a spark of the frenetic energy that always paced in my mind dance into her own. It happened shockingly easily, and she gasped, full lips parting.

Her eyes fluttered gently open, her gaze clear and present. A knot in my belly loosened in relief. Then she smiled, and the ache in my chest increased tenfold.

Chapter Ten

Alyx

I slurped the last of the stew from the flat wooden bowl, my belly pleasantly full. Kelvar glanced at me sidelong, and I thought I saw a flare of satisfaction in his gaze. He had done an impressive job turning the meager supplies he carried with him into a warm meal.

"I didn't know they taught Warlords how to cook," I commented as I set my bowl to the side.

"There is nothing saying we aren't allowed to teach ourselves," he pointed out.

"It seems like a lot to take on, alongside training the riders and doing your Lord's bidding. Besides, what is the point when you are welcome at the Lord's own campfire and can have a share of the choicest meats from every hunt?"

Kelvar shrugged, and I couldn't help but notice the way the muscles of his broad shoulders bunched. He had insisted I keep his robe, and I wrapped it around me, nearly drowning in it even as it shielded me from the sun, leaving him in only a belted vest and loose pants. I could insist on wearing the robe stolen from the fallen rider, but this one smelled like Kelvar.

"You have to be at the encampment to enjoy such privileges," he said, drawing my attention away from the contours of his muscles exaggerated by the deep shadows of late afternoon.

"Are you away from the encampment often?" I asked, cocking my head.

"More often than not."

I frowned. It seemed unusual. Clan Padra's own Warlord shared in my family's stewpot nearly every night, updating his Lord on the training of the riders and any whispers from other clans. I often wished he were away more, thanks to his tendency to sit next to me at the fire, sidling far too close—a behavior I suspected my father encouraged.

"So, you're frequently away kidnapping defenseless daughters for your Lord?" I asked.

Kelvar snorted. "This is actually a first. Normally I'm off to fight a duel in his name or lead a raid on another clan. And I wouldn't call you defenseless. You scared away those attacking riders' horses all on your own. I only felled one of them, while you handled the other two."

I folded my arms, pulling his robe tighter around me. The action brought a wave of his scent to my nose, and I had to make a concerted effort not to inhale deeply. The smell warmed me almost as much as his revelation that I wasn't as helpless as my father seemed to think. Still, I snorted, "You were the one who seemed to think it was laughable when I pointed a knife at you."

Kelvar looked at me thoughtfully, the sun catching in his dark eyes, making their near blackness shine a kaleidoscope of browns and golds. "One can be taught how to hold a knife or wield a sword. Resourcefulness and bravery are harder to impart, both of which you have in spades. You made that clear enough when you endured the storm of my anger without fear. And the raw power that resides in you, well... I've not encountered it's like. Except—"

Kelvar cut himself off, but I knew what he was thinking.

"Except you," I finished for him.

He shook his head. "Not even then. Healing is something I've never been able to master. It's a precious gift. It's no wonder your parents treasure you so."

"It's an odd curse to be protected so closely you're barely allowed to live." The words sprang forth with a vehemence I hadn't known lived within me.

It was Kelvar's turn to frown. "Why did they never teach you to fight or use your power to protect yourself if they were so concerned?"

"You could never heal, and I could never manage even the slightest bit of destruction," I explained. "By the time my parents realized my power was only good for healing, they decided it was too dangerous to have me train with a sword. After all, training with the riders would put me in harm's way."

"And you never fought them on it?"

"I did argue. But I'm not sure I understood the freedom I was missing until—" It was my turn to cut myself off.

Of course, I had *known* the desert was vast and dangerous and beautiful. But it was one thing to be aware, whether through stories or through my magic's sightless sense, and it was another to taste the freedom on the breeze and watch the horizon stretch in every direction with endless possibility.

It was strange to experience liberation through being kidnapped, and I wasn't sure I could ever go back. I shook my head, not willing to entertain those thoughts right now.

"What about you?" I probed instead. "A legendary Warlord, and yet you seem to ask for none of the respect you are due. I've seen your power. You could shake the very foundation of the desert if you dared, but you've never reached for more."

Kelvar turned his face from me, turning toward the fire and throwing another stick on it, though, we no longer needed it for cooking, and the chill of night was hours off yet. "I hadn't found anything that was worth risking what I had already gained."

"Hadn't?" I echoed. "That's changed, though?"

Silence stretched as Kelvar poked at the fire, the crackling of its glowing flames the only noise in the quiet wilderness. He had summoned the fire with a twitch of his fingers, but now he seemed to tend it only to have something to do with his hands.

He didn't respond for long enough that I thought he was going to ignore my question.

Then, murmured so softly it nearly melded with the pop of burning palm fronds, he said, "Perhaps we are teaching each other to dream."

———————⟡———————

I slept through the night and late into the morning of the following day as well. When I woke, sunlight filtered through my eyes a burning red. I raised a hand to shield my face as I squinted, finding myself alone next to the burnt-out embers of the fire.

Sitting up, I looked around for Kelvar and Dileas and found them in the open stretch of sand outside the palms circling the pool of the oasis. I grabbed the spare hood lying in the sand beside me and wrapped it around my head to protect me from the sun before pushing to my feet and picking my way toward them.

Neither of them seemed to notice me as I paused beneath one of the date palms near the outskirts of the oasis. Kelvar stood in the middle of a slightly worn circle, turning on his heel to watch Dileas as she walked around him in a broad arc. He clicked his tongue, and she transitioned to a trot with surprising smoothness. I had known she was a fine horse, but even I had to admit that her gait could compete with my own stallion's.

I tore my eyes away from her shining coat and lovely, long neck to check on her injured leg—or at least, previously injured. From this distance, I could barely even see the scar where her bone had broken through her skin.

A shiver ran up my spine. I had healed broken legs on horses before, but none so seamlessly as Dileas's, especially given how severe her injury had been. It seemed as though my power was closer at hand ever since I had left Clan Padra. Perhaps the vastness of the open desert around me had deepened my connection to her.

Perhaps it was something else.

Kelvar spotted me, and with another click of his tongue, he brought Dileas to a halt. I picked my way out from the shade of the date palm closer to them.

"She's doing well," I remarked.

"Better than I ever could have hoped," he agreed. His dark eyes shone in the light of the bright sun. "And... how are you doing?"

I cocked my head before answering honestly, "Well. I would have expected to feel worse after such a healing."

"You've slept for the better part of two days, and you expected *worse*?"

"My gift is a double-edged sword," I answered with a shrug of my shoulders. "It seems to have a mind of its own."

"I wouldn't know anything about that." Kelvar looked away and scrubbed the back of his neck. The gesture was at odds with the confident, even cocky attitude I had come to expect from him.

"The desert gives and it takes." The words spilled from my lips before I had a chance to think—a refrain so common among the clans that it could serve almost any purpose, from a greeting to a threat. This time though, the meaning hung true. The desert's power was a weighty gift, and both of us had experienced its costs in the past days.

Dileas did not have patience for our reflection, interrupting by nudging her head into my chest with such force I stumbled back a step.

"You're certainly energetic," I commented, reaching up to pat her silky forelock.

"I still want her to rest, but she doesn't seem particularly inclined to stay off her feet," Kelvar huffed.

I turned and walked back toward the oasis, clucking at Dileas over my shoulder. "Come, let's get you some water." Perhaps a nice patch of shade would induce her to relax.

Back near the remnants of our fire from the night before, Kelvar sat on a flat rock at the edge of the clear pool, while Dileas drank her fill. As he did, he reached up to untie a length of cloth around his arm. He hissed as it pulled away from his skin.

I blinked in shock as three deep scratches came into view, cutting across the muscular bulge of his shoulder. I hadn't noticed his injury in all the chaos since the caracals attacked, but my heart leaped into my throat. He had jumped between me and the predators without hesitation.

Edging toward him, I reached out. "Let me help."

Kelvar pulled back, out of my reach, and shook his head. "You don't need to."

"But I—" I chewed my cheek. "I want to."

Kelvar's expression softened fractionally from the grimace of pain etched on it. "These scratches do far less harm than worrying about you lying unconscious for another two days."

Warmth bloomed in my chest and trailed down to my stomach.

"There are ways to help that don't involve magic, you know," I started, still reaching out toward his injuries. "I don't think making sure your cuts are properly cleaned and bandaged will knock me out."

Kelvar hesitated for just a moment then nodded.

I quickly stood, heading to the packs and rifling around for spare cloth I could use. The first thing I found was the thin shift I had been wearing when Kelvar first took me. I mentally shrugged before carrying it over to the oasis and kneeling beside him.

He didn't move, watching quietly as I tore the fabric into strips and soaked a few in the clear water of the oasis. It was cool on my hands, and rivulets dripped down my wrists as I raised the rags toward Kelvar's injured arm. He had done a serviceable job cleaning them, but it must have been difficult to see what he was doing on his own shoulder.

Gently, I dabbed at the area with the cool cloth. Kelvar sucked in a breath through his teeth.

"I'm sorry," I apologized. "Does that hurt?"

He just shook his head. His gaze remained determinedly focused on my hands as I worked.

I leaned closer to get a better view. My knees pressed against his thigh, and the warmth rolling off his skin seeped through my light linen pants. Despite the constant heat shimmering in the air, it wasn't unpleasant.

As the first rag was stained pink from removing the blood crusted on his skin, I reached for a second one. Now, I began cleaning the wounds themselves. While the skin was torn by the rake of the caracal's lethal claws, they didn't seem deep enough to have reached the muscles.

If they had, I might have tried to use just a touch of magic to aid their healing without Kelvar noticing—a task that might have been made difficult by the power dancing and sparking off his skin, leaking into the air around him as if his body wasn't quite large enough to contain it all. The moment I started pulling on threads of power, he would surely sense it.

Instead, I contented myself with making sure no sand or grit had worked its way into the scratches. I leaned so close that my breath stirred the loose hairs that had fallen from the knot at the back of his head to rest on his neck.

Kelvar inhaled sharply again.

My eyes darted to his face, to find his jaw tense, a muscle there ticking as if it took him great effort to hold still.

I turned back to my work, my fingers quickening to complete their task. Two more rags lay stained and discarded beside me by the time I was satisfied. I turned back to my now shredded shift, tearing two more long strips from it. One, I folded to create a sort of pad that would cover all three scratches. The other, I wrapped around his arm to hold the first in place.

Kelvar lifted his arm obligingly so I could wind the bandage behind his shoulder, pulling it tight enough to hold pressure without impeding his movements. As I reached around him, my chest brushed against him, and he let out a hiss that this time I had the wherewithal to realize wasn't pain.

I tried to focus on my task, tying the ends of the bandage off right at the point of his shoulder. My fingers trembled, though, my attention and coordination stolen by the way Kelvar's ribs expanded against me with a shuddering breath.

I rested my hand over his shoulder once I finished, not quite ready to pull away.

"If it festers, I can search for some cara leaves to make a poultice," I murmured, my voice quiet, but still feeling impossibly loud in the tense stillness of the moment. "Or maybe some lyra flowers for the pain."

We both held perfectly still for a moment. I shifted, a quiet voice in the back of my head telling me I needed to pull away.

Kelvar's other arm came to my waist, wrapping around me and keeping me close, and I was all but pressed chest to chest with him. It was my breath that caught this time.

"It hurts less when you touch it," he admitted, a touch of hoarseness edging into his voice.

In response, I traced my fingers lightly over the edge of the cloth, just brushing his skin. The muscles of his shoulder jumped under my touch.

Finally, his gaze tore away from where I had worked on his wound, trailing toward my face, but it snagged on my mouth on its way to my eyes.

My lips parted as I froze, and I found myself leaning closer.

"This is a horrible idea," he murmured.

"We can't," I agreed, my voice just a breath—a puff of air that ghosted over his face as he too leaned in.

"Why not?"

"I don't remember."

The last words were spoken nearly against his lips, and I closed the last of the distance between us. His kiss managed to be gentle and desperate at the same time. Kelvar's arm around my waist pressed me to the hard planes of his chest, even as his lips coaxed mine to open for him with aching sweetness.

My hands tightened on his shoulders, fingers digging into the fabric of his vest and clutching on to him as if I could somehow bring him closer. My head swam, and I couldn't tell if the sparks dancing over my skin were from the dark storm of his power or the touch of his other hand coming to cup the side of my neck. His thumb smoothed back and forth over the hammering pulse in my throat, thundering so loudly I was sure he could hear it.

As I gasped, his tongue slicked into my mouth, and he groaned, the sound broken and ravenous. The hand on my neck moved to my hair, tilting my head gently so he could slot his mouth against mine even more thoroughly.

I wanted—needed—to touch more of him in return. I raked my nails down his chest, scratching across the V of skin visible at the top of his vest.

He sat back, draping me across his lap at the edge of the oasis. His lips dragged from my mouth to my jaw, tongue and teeth exploring down my throat to the sensitive skin behind my ear.

"Tell me to stop," he demanded breathlessly.

"Don't. Please don't stop," I responded, voice already heady with pleasure.

He rewarded me by sucking on the point he had just laved with kisses.

I let my head fall back as a hitched gasp escaped me. My eyes fluttered open to stare sightlessly at the sky, bleached of color by the sun nearing its zenith.

Despite my father's protectiveness, I had managed to steal a handful of kisses with riders of Clan Padra, sometimes accompanied by furtive, wandering hands. But such things had always happened beneath the cover of night, near fires burned down to embers or in the shadows of tents with lowered lanterns.

Out here in the bright of the midday sun, there was no hiding from the blazing heat that Kelvar coaxed to life in my veins. The desert herself watched us, and the glowing plant inside me bloomed as if her magic rejoiced in it.

"You're exquisite, Flower," Kelvar breathed against my skin, causing goosebumps to spread across my arms and down my back, despite the inferno building within me. His words made me wonder if he too could feel the way my magic unfurled in his presence.

His hands moved to the hem of my overlarge tunic, sliding under it to press his palms flat to my stomach. My belly fluttered with anticipation.

"Please," he asked, the word a request and a question all in one.

I swallowed thickly before nodding. As he slipped the fabric over my head and tossed it to the ground beside us, thoughts clambered in the back of my mind, trying to remind me why I shouldn't—*couldn't*—do this. How it could only end in heartbreak—our rival clans pulling us in opposite directions.

But I couldn't make out those voices over the buzz of anticipation and the satisfied purr of my power as Kelvar's gaze roved over my newly bared skin. Even more of his hair had escaped the knot he wore it in, and his lips were already shining and swollen. The armor of the self-assured Warlord was all but cast aside as something equal parts soft and feral filled his eyes.

He only drank me in for a moment before leaning forward and pressing an open-mouthed kiss to my sternum. As his lips traveled sideways, his breath tickling my breast, my hands flew to his hair, pulling it the rest of the way free of its knot. When he took my nipple into his mouth, the gentle tangle of my fingers with his silken strands turned into a hard tug.

He toyed at my breast with his tongue and teeth, and I clapped a hand over my mouth to contain the high-pitched whine that threatened to escape my lips. Kelvar released my breast and shook his head, nuzzling into my skin.

"No one is around for miles, Alyx. Don't deprive me of the noises I work so hard to pull from those pretty lips," he chided.

A huff that might have been a laugh had I had more breath in my chest escaped me. "I didn't think you were working that hard," I gasped, my voice tremulous. Indeed, it seemed that even the slightest touch from him left me ready to fly out of my skin.

"Then I will have to redouble my efforts," he murmured before covering my other breast with his mouth. This time, I did keen as he pressed his flattened tongue to my nipple before worrying it with his teeth.

He grunted in satisfaction, and I arched into his touch, twisting his hair between my fingers. As his mouth explored my chest, his hands drifted down to the sash at my waist, fingers picking at the knot.

My heart jumped to my throat. I had never bared this much of myself to a man. There should be a million reasons why giving myself like this to another clan's Warlord would lead to ruin. I could think of none—only the incessant need curling low in my belly.

I wanted this, and I wanted it with Kelvar.

After all, out here in the open sands with him, I had gained my first taste of freedom. It left me hungry for more, and even hungrier for him.

I helped him slide down my pants, an awkward affair with me still straddling his lap. He smiled, equal parts wicked and sweet as he laid me back on the ground instead, sliding the cloth down my legs. I kicked the garment off, letting it fall in a forgotten pile with my tunic.

Kelvar kneeled between my thighs for a moment, mouth hanging open as he stared at me. The bright sun lit my skin, leaving nothing to the imagination, every divot and valley of my body on display. I might have expected to be shy, bare like this in the unforgiving light of day. The fire in Kelvar's dark eyes burned away any sense of embarrassment I might have had, leaving only simmering need in its wake. I let my own gaze trail over his body—still fully clothed—until it snagged on the visible bulge in the front of his pants. My mouth went dry.

Then Kelvar reached out a hand, trailing the back of his knuckles down the planes of my stomach and between my hipbones to the damp curls at my center. As he trailed lower and parted my folds, I choked, eyes rolling back in my head.

"My Flower's perfect flower, soaked for me."

He lowered himself down, pressing a kiss to my stomach before his lips trailed lower. As they reached the apex of my thighs and his breath tickled my sex, a strangled gasp tore out of me.

"Kelvar."

He raised his eyes to my face expectantly.

I swallowed thickly. "I've never done this," I admitted. I thought I saw a glimmer of fire in his eyes, but it might have just been the sun. He turned and pressed a kiss to my inner thigh, achingly sweet.

"I'll be gentle," he promised, before adding with a crooked grin, "The first time."

My breath caught in my chest. "And the next time?" I asked, barely hoping that such a thing might be possible—that lying with the Warlord trying to hold me for ransom could be more than one wild, reckless taste of freedom.

"Next time, I'll claim you so thoroughly that you'll never want to belong to anybody but me."

I barely had time to register the rush of molten desire his words caused in my veins before his mouth covered my sex. My back arched off the ground as I moaned, but he laid one arm across my hips, keeping me still.

He was good to his word, tongue gently parting my center before moving up to toy with my most sensitive point. I almost wished his touches weren't so tender as my body cried out for *more*.

I was helpless to do anything but gasp and whimper as he worked my pleasure higher with soft caresses. He groaned against my core, as if he were the one being driven to the brink of madness.

Lightning danced behind my eyes as I squeezed them shut against the onslaught of sensation. Instinctually, my magic began to reach out for Kelvar's and found it easily, overwhelming and inescapable in the way its wildness called out to me. I teetered on the edge of a pit of white-hot pleasure, but the moment my own power touched the crackling lightning that danced just beneath Kelvar's skin, I shattered.

A scream escaped me, drowned out by the rumble of thunder in my mind. My thighs trembled beside Kelvar's ears, but he did not relent, the hand between my hip bones pressing me into the ground until all I could do was let out small whines that sounded like begging.

Finally, Kelvar pulled back with one more soft kiss to my inner thigh. I raised my head, barely able to focus my hazy vision on Kelvar. His expression was dazed, as if he were the one who had just broken apart into a million pieces.

"Kelvar," I gasped, my power still dancing with his, unwilling to pull back into the confines of my own skull. I was overwhelmed with pleasure, but still I wanted more.

Kelvar had made me greedy for so many things. For adventure and the endless horizon and him.

"You don't..." he started, even as his hand drifted down to palm his bulging length through his pants.

"I want to," I insisted, voice firm even though I still panted.

Kelvar shrugged out of his own vest before kicking off his pants, and now it was my turn to stare. His tanned skin practically glowed in the sunlight, as if the desert herself bent to his lethal beauty, casting deep shadows under the swell of his pectorals and the divots of his hip bones that accentuated the power of his form.

My mouth grew dry as I followed that V of muscle to the hard length between his legs, and my core fluttered at the way it seemed to strain toward me. Before I could stare too long, Kelvar fell forward, bracing on his elbows and cupping my cheek gently in one of his hands. My eyes snapped up to meet his and found them molten and soft.

He leaned forward to kiss me once more, and I sighed into his mouth at the heartbreakingly gentle press of his lips against mine, even as his steel-hard length rubbed at the sensitized flesh between my legs.

Without pulling his mouth from mine, he slotted against my entrance and pushed just inside. I gasped against his mouth, and he swallowed it down greedily.

My thoughts turned into nothing more than a frenetic buzz, overwhelmed by the onslaught of Kelvar above me, around me, *inside* me. His smell enveloped me, and his magic consumed me and still it wasn't enough. I angled my hips to try and draw him further inside, and it was his turn to gasp as he slid in another inch.

"*Sands*, Alyx," he cursed against my lips. "You feel so perfect around me, it's like you were made for me."

As our magic danced and melded together in my mind, all-consuming in its rightness, I thought he might be right.

He slid in inch by delicious inch until all other rational thought was driven from my mind. With his hips flush against mine, he paused, peppering kisses to my cheeks and forehead while smoothing my hair back from my face with reverent touches.

I couldn't imagine anything more perfect, until he pulled back slightly before driving back in, somehow seating himself even more deeply inside me. My gasp was drowned out by his groan of pleasure. I rolled my hips, urging him to do it again, and he obliged.

Slowly, we found a rhythm, moving against each other in a way that brought tears of pleasure to my eyes. I wrapped my arms around Kelvar and dug my nails into his back, trying to ground myself in this moment even as I felt as if my soul were about to fly out of my body. He ducked his head, panting into my neck as his motions became quicker and more feral.

I urged him on with whimpers of encouragement, every thrust driving the breath from my chest with a high-pitched sound of desperation. He needed no explanation, redoubling his efforts until a sheen of sweat coated both of us.

Another release barreled down on me, as untamed and undeniable as a stampede of wild horses. I buried my face in Kelvar's neck and cried out wordlessly at the intensity of it.

"I know," Kelvar murmured into my ear, his voice as broken as mine. "I know."

I bit down on Kelvar's shoulder, and the copper of blood coated my tongue a moment before I came apart, conscious of nothing but white-hot ecstasy and Kelvar moving within me.

His own groan of release cut through the thunder of blood in my ears, as he buried himself deep inside me one last time, twitching and shuddering with the raw power of his pleasure.

It was long moments before I had the wherewithal to relax my jaw, releasing the tendon between Kelvar's neck and shoulder where I had buried my teeth. I kissed it apologetically as he wrapped his arms around me and rolled to the side, bundling me into his chest.

"I'm sorry," I said, nuzzling the blood-tinged mark again for emphasis as he wrapped his arms around me. I braced my hands on his chest, feeling his heart still hammering under the thick muscle there.

"I'm not," he said, pressing a kiss to the top of my head. "I like that my Flower likes to bite."

"Why do you call me that?" I asked, my voice still breathy from our exertion as I craned my neck to look up at him.

He pulled back to look down at me with darkened eyes.

"Besides the fact that you're the most beautiful thing I've ever seen?" he asked.

A blush would have colored my cheeks if I hadn't already been flushed from head to toe, but I nodded, wanting to hear more.

"Because it's hard to believe something so fine and delicate could exist in the same desert that is full of war and death," he said, the thumb of his hand on my waist tracing a soft circle into my hipbone.

My brows furrowed, and a bolt of annoyance threatened to cut through the pleasant haze I had been drowning in. His words sounded like something my father might say, justifying his suffocating protection. I moved as if to pull my hands away from Kelvar's chest, but one of his own grabbed my wrist, keeping me near as he shook his head.

"But that kind of beauty takes incredible strength. To push back against the conditions that make so much of the desert's flora tough and brittle and choose to be soft and kind."

Kelvar's fingers tightened around my wrist as my breath caught. He lifted it to his lips and pressed a kiss to my palm that liquified my insides.

When he spoke again, his breath tickled the sensitive inside of my wrist. "Your gentle bloom is more powerful than my raging storm."

"Your storm is beautiful too. And a flower can't blossom without a little rain."

Kelvar ducked his head and pressed his forehead to mine, and I knew it was true. I had been drawn to the wild lightning within him the moment I had woken held to his chest. Even as we lay there, sharing breath as our hearts slowed in unison, I worried that I would have to live without it.

The thoughts that had been driven from my mind by Kelvar's proximity—why it was such a catastrophically bad idea to give into the heat between us—finally made themselves known again. Clan Katal's encampment and its waiting Lord lingered over the horizon. There, Kelvar would either have to give me over to his Lord as he was commanded or risk all he had by defying him.

CHAPTER ELEVEN

KELVAR

Alyx slept in my arms through the night for the second time since I had stolen her away, and I prayed to the sands that it would not be the last. At first, I had hoped for this journey with her to be over quickly, but now I wished it to never end. That way, I could keep pretending that there were no reasons for us to keep our distance.

As the sun crested the horizon, I reveled in the stillness of the moments before the desert fully awakened. The often violent and harsh landscape was painted soft and beautiful by the gentle light—everything bleached a silvery gray that seemed to perfectly reflect Alyx's ethereal beauty.

I molded her back even more tightly to my front with the arm flung around her waist and breathed in the flowery scent of her hair. She was so achingly soft in my arms, and even as I reveled in the sleepy peacefulness, I couldn't help the feral hunger it lit for her in my belly.

It was the same desire that had reared its head when Alyx had admitted to me yesterday that she was untouched. It lit a dark possessiveness in me that I was not proud of. I wanted to bind her to me and make her mine forever, even though her beauty and her power were more than anything I had ever even let myself dream of.

Just as I could tell Alyx would no longer be able to go back to her sheltered life in her clan, I knew I would never be able to go back to the simple, destructive existence I had convinced myself was enough.

She stirred in my arms, and I used one hand to gather her hair and push it to one side so I could kiss the curve of her long, elegant neck. She made a sleepy noise of approval, and I couldn't help the way my cock twitched in my pants.

As she wiggled to get closer to me, it ground the curve of her ass against my hardening length, and I nearly swallowed my tongue. Now that I had let my desire off its leash once—let myself have a taste of the perfection that was intimacy with Alyx—I seemed unable to rein it in again.

I thrust against her as the hand over her waist now pressed flat against her belly. Her tunic had rucked up as she slept, and I traced the bare skin around her navel.

"Kelvar," she murmured, letting me know she was awake and aware, even as her voice was still thick with sleep.

I shushed gently, kissing behind her jaw. "Let me take care of you," I said.

She nodded in assent, before letting her head loll back against my shoulder. Her eyes were only half open as she gazed up at me, but her slack face twitched with anticipation as I dipped my fingers below the waistband of her pants. I did not rush their journey to her sex, letting them explore her folds gently and thoroughly, so her breath came in sharp pants by the time I circled her entrance.

Slowly, I slid one finger inside, already finding her wet and ready for my attention. The way she gripped that single digit, though, made my eyes roll back in my head at the memory of how her slick heat had felt around me.

It was good enough to drive me mad.

Carefully, I thrust my finger inside her, earning a high whimper as my palm ground against her most sensitive point. She squirmed, as if seeking out more contact. I obliged, bringing my other hand up to cup one of her breasts. I massaged it before rolling her nipple between my fingers through her clothing.

She twitched in pleasure, and I reveled in how sensitive and responsive she was.

I continued my attentions for long moments, rubbing her heated flesh as I stretched her open with another finger. I drank in the hitches of her breath and the flush that traveled down her cheeks to her neck as if she were an oasis and I were dying of thirst.

Finally, her moans and whimpers shaped into words once more. "I want you inside me again," she insisted.

"I am inside you, Flower," I pointed out, thrusting my fingers for emphasis.

She squirmed in my hold and huffed indignantly. "Kelvar."

There was nothing I wouldn't give her when she asked so prettily. I removed my hand from her breast and used it to shove my pants down my hips until my already throbbing cock sprang free. She helped me, shimmying her own pants down her legs. They went easily, several sizes too big as they were.

Even as I ached to replace my fingers with my throbbing length, it took great effort to pull them free of her exquisite heat. I could touch her forever.

I managed it though, instead using that hand to part her thighs, holding her top leg up to give me access to her center. With a few circles of my hips, I slicked up my length in the nectar already coating her inner thighs.

She sighed in pleasure, and I let my free hand come to her neck, arching her back so I could kiss her as I slid inside. Alyx whimpered into my mouth, and the sound set my skin aflame. I had meant to be gentle as I worked inside her waiting heat, but my hips snapped forward involuntarily, stretching her around my length. I nipped her lower lip and murmured an apology.

"I'll be gentle," I promised.

She shook her head, even as her chest heaved with shuddery breaths. "You promised next time you'd claim me so thoroughly that I would never belong to anybody else."

The reminder of my words made my cock twitch. But still I hesitated. I had meant to bring her to soft, gasping pleasure in my arms this morning. To wake her gently with kisses and promises that I might not be able to keep.

She rolled her hips against mine, and those rational thoughts left my brain as a primal instinct screamed at me to bury myself as deep inside her as possible.

"Remember, I'm tougher than I look, and you have the bite mark to prove it," she murmured, her voice already cracked with pleasure.

She was right. I had admired the mark in my reflection in the oasis pool the night before.

"If you're sure," I said, the bite on my neck throbbing happily as I parted her legs further, giving me more access to drive into her.

"Make me yours," she insisted.

And I couldn't deny her anything. My hips snapped forward. A sharp gasp of pleasure escaped her as I kept her in place with my hand at her throat. I didn't squeeze, but my fingers around her neck kept her face tipped back where I could devour her mouth as I drove into her.

Her pale lashes fluttered as I thrust again and again, gaining speed. She clenched and shuddered around me, but I wanted more. I wanted *everything*.

Even my magic tried to burrow in her even more deeply. My storm twisted with the tendrils of light that spilled from her until they seemed to meld together. They had never fully untangled since our joining last night, but now they melded until I did not know where my power ended and hers began. Perhaps they weren't even different at all.

I hooked her top leg around my hip, leaving her thighs spread obscenely wide and freeing my hand to explore her as I pleased. It drifted to where I entered her, tracing the way her folds stretched around my length as I drove into her with increasing force.

As my fingers slid to her sensitive bud once more, she tightened around me, and I grunted through the frisson of pleasure it sent up my spine.

"Sands Alyx," I growled. "I can't wait to feel you come apart."

She whimpered in response. I thrust harder and faster, trying to draw even more noises from her as I timed the circles of my fingers over her flesh with my movements. She obliged, louder and more desperate sounds ripping from her as I pounded into her exquisite heat.

She began to tremble, and I tightened my hand around her throat, not enough to restrict her air flow, but enough to pin her in place as I made her come apart.

Alyx shattered with a sharp cry, and her vice grip on my cock tightened so far that my vision whited out. Still, I did not relent, burying myself in her again and again and continuing to stroke her sensitized flesh. As her pleasure faded, she squirmed and whimpered, both trying to get closer and escape the onslaught of sensations.

"Be good and come for me one more time," I insisted. My voice barely sounded like my own, coming out in an otherworldly growl, unintentionally laced with magic and rumbling like storm clouds on the horizon.

Alyx gasped, and her eyes, which had been screwed shut in pleasure, snapped open. Her head craned back so she could meet my gaze, and it transfixed me. I was helpless to do anything but bury myself in her welcoming flesh, desperate to drag her pleasure from her again. It was as if I could feel her ecstasy barreling down on her, or maybe that was just my own.

The fire crackling in my veins roared to life with the strength of an inferno, rushing up my spine and out my mouth as I roared my own release. Alyx matched me with a scream of her own, coming apart around me, and I could barely separate my pleasure from hers as we shook and shuddered.

As my breath slowed, and the trembling in my limbs slowly abated, I lowered my head to nuzzle in the junction between her neck and shoulder. My hand at her neck drifted down to her chest, pressing flat over her breastbone. Her heart hammered under my fingers, synchronized with my own.

Her breath hitched, and I felt it too. Even as my cock slipped from inside her, as I repositioned to hold her to me more comfortably, our magic did not pull apart. It was now knotted together so thoroughly that I wasn't sure I could disentangle it without hurting one or both of us—I wasn't sure I even desired to tease it apart.

If the way Alyx turned in my arms to burrow herself into my chest was any indication, she was not inclined to either. As she nuzzled into my sternum, I had the fleeting thought that she hadn't just stolen my heart... she *was* my heart.

Alyx stood by Dileas, the unsure way she stroked the mare's flank echoing my own hesitance. With all of us healed, there was no reason to forestall our journey, but the destination that had been so clear before now seemed clouded.

The simple transaction I had once imagined when arriving back at Clan Katal's encampment now made bile rise in my throat. Alyx was not a simple prisoner I would allow Lord Deryn to ransom back to her father where she would live under his suffocating shelter.

An uncomfortable twisting in the strange magical tether that now existed between us told me that Alyx feared this eventuality as well. I strode over to her, covering her hand with mine where it wound in Dileas's mane.

"I will not hand you over to Lord Deryn," I promised without preamble.

She looked up at me, her expression equal parts hopeful and sad. "And what will you do instead? Defying your Lord could cost you everything."

I swallowed around the feeling of glass in my throat. I had come from nothing to be the most powerful Warlord in the Ballan Desert, and I had always avoided wanting more for fear of losing what I had. But Alyx—she was worth risking all of it. I would gamble existence itself for her.

"I have served my Lord loyally and without question for many years," I insisted. "He will allow me this one thing."

"And if he does not?"

"I am more powerful than he, and he will learn," I promised darkly.

Alyx nodded, but I did not miss the flicker of apprehension in her eyes before she looked away. Even when the riders of Clan Tibel had attacked, and I would have had no issue killing them all and skinning them for her pleasure in punishment for daring to touch her, she had chosen a different path. She had kept them alive, finding an alternative to spilling blood while still protecting herself.

The violence that came so easily to me was not in her nature, and I could not bring myself to want to change that. I tried to distract her from thoughts of bloodshed.

"When Lord Deryn does agree to let you stay at my side, I'll move into a larger tent where we will be comfortable together. I'll show you how well I can actually cook when I don't just have my meager traveling supplies. And the Clan will welcome a healer of your skill," I declared.

At this, she did smile. "I look forward to it."

Chapter Twelve

Alyx

Mountains appeared on the horizon, stretching farther and farther up toward the sky the closer we rode. I had seen the peaks bordering the desert before, but rarely had I come this close. Still, we rode nearer

The scent of woodsmoke and the yips of hunting dogs signaled that we approached an encampment. Almost a week of riding without Kelvar's clan in sight, and now it appeared only a day's ride from the oasis where we had rested.

My spine stiffened as I sat before Kelvar on his horse, approaching the large circle of tents in the distance, nestled right into the base of the mountains. Despite his assurances that he would make his Lord see reason, the threat of violence remained palpable in the air. Dread filled my belly, heavy and potent at the thought of bloodshed on my behalf.

But I trusted Kelvar.

As we passed through the first ring of tents, it was as if a shadow fell over us, and my sense of foreboding grew. Clan encampments were usually full of life, from children playing to horses nickering. While Clan Katal's camp was not quiet, there was the undertone of tense anticipation in all the voices drifting on the air.

Kelvar sensed it too, if the way his harm tightened around my waist was any indication. Still, he sat proudly and did not slow his mount as we headed toward the tallest tent in the encampment: Lord Deryn's. It stood just at the base of the mountain, shadowed by the peaks looming over head.

We reached the clear area surrounded by the largest tents, and I frowned as people abandoned their fires and ducked out of their own dwellings to watch. While Clan Padra's Warlord was often greeted with cheerful waves and shouts of greeting when he returned from a battle, Clan Katal watched Kelvar warily. It was as if they feared his power. I wondered if that was why Lord Deryn sent him away so often.

We stopped in front of the largest tent. At the top, the banner bearing the black and white viper of Clan Katal flapped in the wind.

The dread that had bubbled sluggishly in my belly boiled up into my throat. I shrank back into Kelvar, almost wanting to suggest that we turn and leave.

But he was determined. He hopped down from Dileas's back and approached Lord Deryn's tent. Before he could reach the entrance flap, Lord Deryn himself emerged. He stood a few inches taller than Kelvar, but where Kelvar's shoulders were wide and imposing, Lord Deryn's bare arms were wiry and lithe. His shaved head reflected the evening sun, revealing swirling lines inked over his bare scalp.

"You took long enough," he greeted Kelvar without preamble.

I frowned. It did not seem wise to treat somebody so powerful with such disdain. But Kelvar did not seem perturbed, almost as if he were used to the treatment.

He wrapped his knuckles to his temple in a sign of respect to his Lord as he answered. "The desert was challenging," he admitted, "But she has rewarded us with a great gift."

Lord Deryn's gaze drifted to me where I still sat atop his horse. Dileas pawed at the ground, and I tried to sit proudly.

"The spawn of Lord Avis will fetch us a mighty price indeed. He is notoriously weak when it comes to his daughter," he sneered.

The way he looked at me set my teeth on edge, but Kelvar cut in before I could think to speak.

"We will not be ransoming her back to her father," he declared.

Lord Deryn's face purpled, but Kelvar pushed on as if he hadn't noticed.

"I will be marrying Alyx, and her healing abilities will make her an invaluable asset to our people."

I almost fell off his horse at the sudden declaration. While he had made it clear that he would keep me at his side, this was the first time he had mentioned marriage. But as he glanced back at me, I couldn't help the beginning of a smile that quirked my lips at the thought—at the way he barreled into a future with me with no second thoughts or hesitation.

Lord Deryn spluttered and spat. "I have no use for a healer! We need a weaponsmith, one her father will surely allow us to take for his daughter's safe return."

Kelvar's fingers drifted toward the hilt of his saber, but still, he tried to reason. "I have never asked much of you, my Lord. I have let you command my power as you willed—wield me as a weapon against your foes. I am asking you to grant me this one wish. Let me make Alyx my wife."

I didn't see the men creeping up on my side until it was too late. Dileas reared in response to my sudden panic, lashing out with her lethal hooves. As her actions caused me to slip back, one of the men grabbed me by the leg and yanked. I slipped from Dileas's back and hit the baked earth with a thud so hard it made my eyes water.

"Alyx!" Kelvar screamed.

Before I could clear my swimming vision, a heavy boot landed between my shoulder blades, keeping me pinned face first in the dirt. Unable to move or get to my feet, I lifted my head, finding Kelvar, sword drawn and staring at me with murder in his eyes. I didn't even need the strange connection between us to feel the way his magic roiled and raged, ready to explode out in an almighty wave.

He could level this camp. He could kill everybody in this clearing with a swipe of his arm. I had seen the destructive power that lurked under his skin. Kelvar could save me, but at a price I was not willing to pay.

"Wait!" I shouted around a mouthful of dust. I said the word out loud at the same time as I tugged on the strange tether between us. Kelvar stiffened, as did everybody else in the large audience that had now gathered to watch the commotion.

"A duel," I panted. "Such matters should be decided with a duel of honor."

I couldn't live with the all-out destruction of this clan on my behalf, but one clean death could buy peace.

Lord Deryn sneered, "And why would I agree to this duel when I have already gained what I want?" He nodded at me where I lay on the ground.

I tried to push to my hands and knees, but the man with the boot on my back bore down harder, grinding his heel into my spine painfully. I gasped, and lightning crackled in the air as Kelvar's anger flared.

"Do you truly think your men would still live if your Warlord wished them dead?" I asked, even as my voice was thin with pain. "They are only alive by my mercy. Because I haven't told Kelvar to kill them yet."

Lord Deryn blanched, and the pressure on my back lessened slightly.

"If you refuse to duel with Kelvar, you may as well admit that he is more skilled than you," I continued. "And strength is the highest law of the Ballan Desert. Refuse to duel him, and you are admitting you are an unfit Lord."

He bristled, but the murmuring of the crowd around us told me I had hit a nerve. Kelvar had only been controlled by his disinterest in more power. But just as I was no longer going to allow anybody to deny me my freedom, he would no longer be a weapon.

Neither of us could be controlled anymore.

A metallic *shink* marked Lord Deryn drawing his blade and turning it toward Kelvar. "A dual of honor it is. No magic, just our skill with a blade," he agreed. I almost admired the bravery in his firm tone, but it wasn't quite enough to hide the trembling of his hands. Kelvar was a fearsome opponent, and duals in the desert only ended one way.

"The victor will be the Lord of Clan Katal, and the desert will drink the blood of the defeated and be sated," Kelvar declared.

"The desert gives, and it takes," Lord Deryn agreed.

Everybody in the vicinity backed away as Lord Deryn began to circle, creating an open space for their battle. I found myself dragged backward by the man who had pinned me down. I scrabbled back on my hands, barely noticing as I refused to rip my gaze from Kelvar.

While the Lord circled him, searching for openings, Kelvar remained preternaturally still, simply pivoting in place. His feet were planted, and he held his over-long saber before him with its tip pointed at the ground.

He seemed nearly unprepared, like an easy target. But his magic was pulled taut, like a bowstring ready to spring forward with lethal efficiency.

Lord Deryn sprang forward, incomprehensibly fast. Kelvar was faster, though, stepping to the side and throwing his own blade out. Lord Deryn was barely able to stay his momentum enough to avoid slicing himself in half.

He stumbled, and Kelvar pressed the advantage, pushing forward with a flurry of blows. Lord Deryn got his saber up in time to block them, and sparks flew from the clash of their blades, dancing in the deepening twilight.

I gasped as Lord Deryn managed to parry one of Kelvar's blows, shoving it aside and creating an opening. He stabbed forward, straight at Kelvar's chest. But Kelvar moved inconceivably fast for his size, lunging sideways and ducking low. The blow whistled over his head, and he came up under Lord Deryn's guard.

The crowd hissed in unison as Kelvar slammed the pommel of his saber into Lord Deryn's face. His head snapped back and he stumbled away, blood streaming from his nose. Kelvar advanced, and I could feel the thrill of battle singing in his blood second hand, but still enough to be all-consuming and intoxicating.

Kelvar fought like I healed: With every fiber of his consciousness.

He swung his saber down in a brutal overhead strike. Lord Deryn lifted his weapon just in time to defend himself, and their hilts caught. They bore down on each other, limbs shaking and teeth bared. Lord Deryn was taller, but Kelvar's added bulk made him difficult to overcome.

Kelvar gained the upper hand, driving Lord Deryn to his knees, but he still didn't let his guard drop. Instead, a potent mix of fear and fury sparked in Deryn's eyes.

"I was the one who recognized your power, and you thank me by betraying me for some woman," he hissed.

"She's not just some woman," Kelvar growled in response.

Their words distracted me enough that I didn't notice Lord Deryn letting go of his saber with one hand and sneaking it into his boot. Kelvar was able to push aside his sword, with only one hand holding the guard. But Lord Deryn already had what he needed.

His wrist snapped forward and he threw a lethal silver blade straight at my face. Time seemed to slow as it flew toward me. I tried to dive out of the way, but the rider who had grabbed me still held me in place.

Kelvar spun toward me and threw out his hand. Magic crackled as he reached out, grabbing the thrown knife with his power. It stopped in midair, quivering, but my moment of relief was short lived.

Pain bloomed in my mind and Kelvar howled. The knife thudded to the ground harmlessly, but in his moment of distraction, Deryn had struck Kelvar's outstretched arm. Blood bloomed from a gash on the inside of his elbow, deep enough to have cut through his muscles and tendons.

His sword arm hung uselessly at his side. The fire of victory lit in Lord Deryn's eyes, but Kelvar's fury shattered. He grabbed his dirk from his belt with his off hand. Lord Deryn struck, but with Kelvar's full rage unleashed, he was too slow. Kelvar caught the blade in the handguard of his dirk and twisted it out of the way. In the same movement, he lunged forward, driving the blade deep into Lord Deryn's eye.

Blood sprayed, covering his arm and wrist as he drove the dirk into the hilt and twisted savagely. Lord Deryn's breath left him with a shuddered gasp as he went limp, and Kelvar wrenched his blade free.

The corpse toppled to the ground, and silence descended over the clearing, the only sound Kelvar's ragged breathing. In the extended moment of shocked stillness, I managed to wrench myself away from the grasp of the rider who held me. I scrabbled through the sand to get to Kelvar, who swayed where he stood.

I needed to check the extent of his injuries. I needed to throw myself into his arms and breath in his scent—tangle in the threads of his magic to assure myself he had survived. Finally, I stood before him and cupped his face in my hands, looking into the deep pools of his eyes. I found sparks dancing in their depths.

A smile quirked the edge of his lips, and despite the way my fingers itched to reach for his wound and knit it back together, I smiled back at him. We had survived.

His dirk fell from his good hand, forgotten in the dust, and he interlaced his fingers with my own. Turning me toward the onlookers, he raised our interlaced hands high.

"Would anybody else like to challenge my right to be Lord of Clan Katal and marry this woman?"

The assembled clan and riders raised their hands and tapped their knuckles to their foreheads in respect. I sighed in relief, but it quickly turned into a frown.

Kelvar heard it the same second I did, his hand tightening in mine. Hoofbeats, enough for dozens of horses. Then the screams started.

"A raid!" Kelvar shouted. "Find cover!"

Horses crashed into the encampment, their riders swinging their sabers and screaming out bloodcurdling war cries. The people of Clan Katal scattered, riders drawing weapons as those who weren't warriors ran for shelter.

Kelvar dragged me behind him with his uninjured arm and tried to lift his sword before him with the other. It trembled, and the point only raised a few degrees from the ground, even as he grunted in effort. His tendons must be severed, not allowing the limb to respond to his commands.

"You can't fight!" I insisted.

"It will take more than this scratch to keep me from protecting you," he said gravely.

I tried to drag him out of the fray, but he planted his feet. Kelvar growled savagely at the incoming onslaught, pinning me between him and the Lord's tent at my back. Against the mountain as it was, we wouldn't be able to retreat that way.

Then, icy dread spread through my veins as two familiar horses crashed into the open circle: My father and his Warlord. Savagely, they cut down Clan Katal's riders, who by now had managed to draw weapons and mount a resistance. With the thick knot of riders that had gathered in the center of the encampment to watch the duel, the attacking warriors of Clan Padra were considerably slowed.

"Stop!" I shouted, but my voice couldn't be heard over the cacophony of clanging steal and angry shouts.

Bile rose into my throat as my father swung his saber in a downward slash, catching a woman who wielded a pair of sickle blades against him across the shoulder. Her scream of pain pierced my heart as she fell to her knees in the sand, already wet with blood.

Kelvar must have shared my distress at the bloodshed of his people, and a pulse of rage traveled through me, although I could not tell if it was my own or from the magical tether running between us. He let go of me with his good hand and threw it out. His magical slash caught one of Clan Padra's attacking riders across the chest, and he fell from his horse with a shriek. The crunch of him hitting the ground cut through the sound of battle, and I felt it in my own bones.

Both of these Clans were my people.

I didn't have time to dwell on it, as Kelvar's actions had drawn my father's attention. Catching sight of Kelvar, and me behind him, he spurred his horse toward us with a roar.

"Give back my daughter, you snake!" he shouted, voice booming over the din of battle. He raised his blade as he charged through the mayhem, ready to slash down in a blow that would cleave Kelvar's skull in two if it landed.

Kelvar tried to raise his saber to block, but he wouldn't be able to with his injured arm. His uninjured hand raised, and the earthy smell of magic filled the air around me.

One thought filled my head as I leaped into motion: I could not let more blood be spilled on my account.

Chapter Thirteen

Kelvar

One moment, I stared down the charging Lord of Clan Katal, ready to cut him from his horse as his blade swung down. The next second, Alyx was between us, the sword headed straight for her chest.

Magic had already gathered in my mental grasp, but panic snapped every vestige of control I had. Power detonated out of me, screaming in my ears and turning my vision white.

It was long moments before I could see again, and my ears still rang as I blinked stars from my vision, desperately trying to focus on Alyx. My gaze found her easily, as she was the only person that remained standing in the clearing where battle had been waging on. Everybody lay on the ground as if knocked over by an earthquake. Lord Avis had fallen from his mount and was sprawled at Alyx's feet.

He blinked dazedly, until his eyes focused on his daughter's face. I could not see it, as she stood with her back turned to me, but I could see the steely determination written in the set of her shoulders. It reverberated through the bond between us.

"Alyx!" he shouted as he gained back his breath. "Stand aside and let me dispatch this kidnapper." He tried to struggle to his feet, saber still clutched in his hand.

"No," she said firmly. "He is not a kidnapper. I am choosing to stay with Clan Katal."

Lord Avis's lips drew back from his teeth in a snarl. "He's hood-winked you, and you're too naïve to realize it. Get out of the way and let me free you from his influence."

My hackles rose, and the magic that was still close at hand after the giant shockwave I had let out began to crackle in my veins. It burned me from the inside out, and I itched to use it on a parent who would so casually dismiss a daughter so kind and wise as Alyx.

"Listen to me, father," she insisted. "I will not have you spill blood on my behalf when my decision is final."

All the other people in the clearing now staggered to their feet, but they did not begin fighting again, all watching how this confrontation would play out.

"You do not command Clan Padra," he scoffed. He was on his feet again, and he raised his saber, the tip angled toward Alyx. At the sight, the power that had been whispering in my mind grew in volume, hammering at the inside of my head as if desperate to escape.

I grit my teeth against it and tried to step around Alyx to put myself between her and the blade. She turned though, maneuvering so she still stood between us with one hand outstretched at each of us placatingly.

I lifted my chin and growled at Lord Avis, "Maybe she would be a wiser commander than you."

Anger flashed in his eyes. "I will not stand for this insult. Clan Padra will attack Clan Katal again and again if we must, until your memory is wiped from the sands."

"I will level your entire encampment if I have to," I rumbled, sparks beginning to dance at my fingertips. It was not an empty threat. Somehow, more power was bubbling in me than ever had before.

My magic waxed and waned with the desert's will—granting me strength whenever there was something particularly important she wanted done. If she wanted me to turn every rider of Clan Padra to a red stain on the sand to keep Alyx safe, I would.

Alyx's voice cut through the haze beginning to cloud my vision. "It will never end, will it? There is nowhere in the desert we can be free and live in peace together, is there?"

Even as she stood between us, her voice held so much sadness that I heard my heart crack. She had made me dream of more. She had believed in me and told me that I could shake the very foundations of the desert if I dared, but in all that bottomless power, I could not give her peace.

The power of the desert pulsed in my mind, as if trying to get my attention. I frowned, turning my focus inward to the storm roiling in my chest. It spread out through my limbs and began spilling off my skin in tremulous waves.

"Kelvar," Alyx said, sounding concerned as the ground began to shake. She stepped toward me, even as others in the clearing began backing away. Lord Avis hesitated, but the shadow of fear now darkened his eyes.

Still, I did not stop. I dived headfirst into the storm, and the rumbling of the ground intensified. But the desert in my mind urged me forward. I could give Alyx the peace and the freedom she deserved if I just dug deep enough. For Alyx, I dared to shake the foundations of the desert, and I would remake it in her vision. I would craft her a place where she could be free and safe.

I fell to my knees and laid the palm of my uninjured hand flat on the ground, trying to get as close to the desert as possible, even as she swam inside me. Everybody but Alyx began running from the clearing. Screams and shouts sounded, but they all blended into the screech of my magic.

"Kelvar!" Alyx cried, falling to her knees beside me and putting her hands on my shoulders.

I shook my head.

"For you, Flower. All for you," I grit out, before my consciousness completely shattered.

I *was* the desert and her shifting sands. I lived in every rock and every creature, all woven together in a complicated web.

And at the edge of that beautiful tapestry, I envisioned a place of peace and beauty. A home where all would be welcome and peace would reign. I thought of Alyx's smile and the way she shattered apart in my arms. I thought of her softness and quiet strength and the way she had made me *dream*.

I imagined a place made of all those things, and I didn't relent until the desert bent to my will.

Time lost all meaning to me, but eventually a familiar touch brought me back to myself. Gently fingers traced along my cheekbones and soft, warm breath feathered across my face.

It reminded me that I had a face and body to come back to, when all I could feel was the tangled web of life and death that spread from the mountains to the ocean.

"You did it Kelvar. You can come back now."

The voice whispered sweetly in my mind and in my ears. Sound filtered in after touch, and I realized the world had gone quiet after constant rumbling and shouting.

"Alyx," I murmured, regaining control of my movements.

"I'm here," she confirmed, her thumbs stroking my cheekbones more insistently.

Finally, my eyes opened—opened to find her pale, silvery eyes filled with tears.

"There you are." She sighed in relief.

"I'd never leave you," I promised.

A breathy laugh of relief escaped her. "I have no doubt. You reshaped the very fabric of the desert for me."

Now I blinked. Thinking of the place I had imagined—a home for me and Alyx.

"Did I..."

Alyx moved from my line of sight, instead sitting down next to me where I still kneeled in the sand. I faced the mountains, but no longer were they just a steep slope of gray rock climbing up toward the sky. Sprouting from the mountainside, were geometric squares. As I blinked in confusion, my vision started to organize itself.

Buildings and roads all stacked on top of each other, climbing up from the foot of the mountain. A city that could house hundreds—thousands—carved straight into the rock. The concentric layers climbed upward to an incredible palace, from the top of which emerged a tower with an impressive spire. From there, one would be able to look out over the whole desert. I even imagined you could see the ocean sparkling on the horizon, though, I knew it to be hundreds of miles away.

My mouth hung open as I let my gaze drift down over the geometric architecture to the sight immediately before us. Encircling the brand new city was a high wall, carved out of the same stone as every other bit of it. It appeared completely solid and unbroken, presenting a beacon of absolute safety, apart from the large, arched entrance directly in front of where Alyx and I kneeled.

I scrabbled to my feet in shock. Alyx stood next to me and slid her hand into my own. If her delicate fingers had not squeezed mine so reassuringly, I might have thought it was a dream. My boots seemed rooted to the ground, but she tugged me forward.

"Let's go look," she prompted.

I stared at her, dumbfounded. She just smiled.

"Can we?" I asked dumbly.

She nearly laughed, but she seemed just as dazed as I was.

"You pulled this marvel from the mountainside. I don't know why we wouldn't be able to," she pointed out.

I let her tug me along. We passed under the stone archway, and something deep in my gut shivered at the magnitude of the stone around us. The familiar feel of sand giving way underfoot turned into the harsh slap of my boots against solid rock as we entered a large courtyard. Branching out from it were paths in a variety of directions, along with one large road, climbing up and up through the stacked stone levels toward the palace at the top.

I stood in the center of it all and pivoted in place, taking in my surroundings. My heart stuttered. Alyx had made me believe I could do anything, but even I had not imagined this until the desert had whispered in my mind to try it. But I had wanted a home for Alyx, and so it had become.

A growing wave of whispers and voices distracted me. I had nearly forgotten that we had been surrounded by other people—people who had fled the vicinity when the ground started to heave and shake with my efforts to reshape it.

Now, they hesitantly approached the open archway into the new city. At the front of the crowd stood Lord Avis. His eyes were wide and his mouth hung open. I understood the feeling of shock written on his expression, but I raised my chin. I pulled Alyx closer and exchanged my hand in hers for putting my left arm protectively around her waist.

My right arm still hung uselessly by my side, but such things barely seemed to matter right now. I hardly knew what to do with this new place I had wrought—with the fact that I could accomplish such a thing—but Alyx smiled up at me, and nothing else mattered. She was wise and kind, and I trusted her.

"Come in!" she shouted, beckoning to those who hesitated outside the arch. Slowly, the group trickled in and looked around in awe. I watched the riders warily, knowing they had been fighting just before I had gone into my trance, although it felt like lifetimes ago. The change in events seemed to have at least temporarily sapped the fight from them, though.

"What is this place?" Lord Avis asked first, stopped several meters from where I stood with Alyx.

She looked at me, and I nodded to her. This place was for her, and it could be whatever she wished it to be, as long as she and I could share it.

"This is a new beginning," she declared, loud enough for all the gathering crowd to hear. "This new city will be a place where any rider of the desert can be at home and the divisions between clans disappear."

She trailed off as titters ran through the crowd, but the hazy vision that had driven me forward as I shaped the rock became solid and real. "This will be a place of peace," I shouted. "And all those who try to bring war within its walls will answer to me."

The shuffling of feet and unsure glances people shared told me that no one here today would be quick to cross me after such a display. Still, Alyx turned her face to me and beamed. Dirt smudged and rumpled as she was, she already glowed like a queen, and I could think of no better gift for her than her own kingdom.

Now she spoke, confident and sure, all traces of the stifled woman I had abducted burned away with her power. "This great city shall be ours, and we will call it Kelvadan."

EPILOGUE

ALYX

T he desert was beautiful at sunset.

It was my favorite time of day to stand on the balcony at the highest room of the tower in the palace at Kelvadan. Kelvar had claimed it as our bedroom as soon as we reached it while exploring the structure for the first time.

From here, I could see the sands stretching endlessly in every direction, full of promise, and the solidity of the mountains protected my back. Riding across the dunes with Kelvar had made me crave the openness of the horizon, and he had gifted it to me—both the security of a home and the freedom of endless possibilities.

Now I stood with my back to our new room, sparsely furnished as we were still settling in, and looked out at the city below us. We weren't the only ones still getting used to our new homes. The streets were sparsely populated, mostly with a handful of riders from Clans Katal and Padra who had chosen to stay in the new city. My father had ridden off with the rest of Clan Padra, and a rider Kelvar trusted took command of the remainder of Clan Katal.

Still, more and more clansmen from the other seven clans trickled in by the day. Some were simply curious, while others had an inkling they would be better suited to a stationary home than their current nomadic situations. I had even met a few other couples from mixed clan backgrounds when I walked through the city.

Already, I loved wandering the streets and talking to the new citizens, helping them adjust to the new ways of life and lending a healing hand when I could. Several clans had stopped by the new city and brought me their ill and wounded, and something in me blossomed at the opportunity to serve the desert and *all* her clans like this.

I could scarcely believe that Kelvar had given me all this.

As if summoned by my thoughts, he joined me on the balcony. His arms wound around my waist, and I leaned back into his chest. I was glad to feel their strength after spending almost a full day unconscious from healing his injured arm. Even then, I had insisted on checking it daily, ensuring I had knit his muscles and tendons together just right.

"And how is my queen this evening?" Kelvar asked now, leaning down to speak the words right into the shell of my ear.

I wrinkled my nose, even as the tickle of his breath sent shivers down my spine.

"I still feel odd being called that," I admitted. Neither Kelvar nor I had declared ourselves a king or a queen. We had simply moved into the palace and said any were welcome to call the city home. But as we began helping the citizens and mediating the inevitable disputes, people began using the titles automatically.

I still blushed and stammered when somebody attached the honorific to my name, and I sensed Kelvar enjoyed it, finding every excuse possible to call me *Queen Alyx*.

"It's what you are though," he insisted now. "You've been my queen ever since the first time I laid eyes on you. And now you have a city with which to share your bravery and beauty."

I shook my head. "I can't believe you did this for me."

"I'd rip the foundations of the earth asunder for you if I had to," he promised. "I still can't believe you insisted on naming it after me."

I turned in his arms, putting my hands flat on his chest. "I want everyone to see your greatness when they look at this city. I want this to be a testament to your power—evidence of the beauty of that storm that lives beneath your skin, that everybody will remember for centuries to come."

"But it's not." Kelvar shook his head, using his hand on my lower back to pull me flush against him. My stomach fluttered despite how often this had happened in the past few weeks. "This is not a testament to my power but to my love for you. If I had had my way, I would have named it after *you*. So, a good long while from now, when we pass this same city to our children, and their children, and their children's children, they will all look at it in awe and say, 'Never before has a man so loved his wife.'"

"Our children?" I asked with a hitch in my breath.

I did not miss the way Kelvar's magic shivered as I said the word, and mine twitched in return. The entanglement of our power only seemed to grow deeper by the day, and I had no desire to pull it apart—I wasn't even sure it would be possible.

Kelvar smiled with mischief, and the warmth that had already been growing in my blood dripped down my spine at the expression.

"Yes," he insisted, leaning forward and kissing my neck. "Someday, I'll give you as many children as you desire. And I will enjoy making them immensely."

The liquid desire pooling in my gut caught fire at the thought. "Show me," I tried to demand, although my voice came out breathless. "Show me just how much you'll enjoy it."

Kelvar nipped at my earlobe, and I felt him smile against my neck. "Of course, my queen."

The next thing I knew, my feet left the ground, Kelvar's hands under my thighs hoisting me into the air. I let him carry me, trusting in his strength as I tried to distract him with my lips on his jaw and my hands plunging into his hair.

He huffed against my skin in amusement at my enthusiasm, laced with a hefty amount of his own desire. Once he deposited me on the bed, he stared down at me for a moment. My hair spread around me, and I beamed broadly before reaching up for him. But he shook his head, instead lowering his hands to my thighs where the nightgown I had donned for bed had ridden up.

"I want to see you," he insisted, sliding it up before lifting it over my head and tossing it to one side.

"You too," I challenged, raising my chin at him. He wasted no time stripping off his own tunic and pants. In the fiery orange light of the rapidly setting sun, he seemed bathed in fire—all hard lines and lethal grace. He was the dangerous beauty of the desert incarnate, and he was mine.

Now I drew him down to me, and he did not resist, dipping his head to devour my mouth. I sighed as his scent and warmth enveloped me, even as his hard length against my hip lit something primal in me.

I bucked against him, trying to gain friction. Kelvar responded by snaking one hand between us while the other tangled in my hair and held me still.

"You know I'll take care of you, Flower," he chided, slowly tracing my sex. I squirmed, nearly embarrassed by the slickness he found already gathered there. But he smiled as his fingers slipped through my folds, and if the way his cock strained toward me was any indication, his desire was just as urgent.

Still, he slowly stroked me, to the point I was nearly blind with pleasure before he removed his fingers. Finally, he replaced his hand with his hard length and began sliding inside. I threw my head back and gasped, still made breathless by the stretch.

It was perfect.

When he finally worked himself all the way inside and began to move, I wrapped my legs around his powerful hips, and we both gasped at the way it angled him impossibly deeper. His hands were everywhere—pushing my hair away from my face, stroking my cheeks, trailing down my sides, and leaving goosebumps in their wake.

It was so much, but I would never have enough of Kelvar.

I closed my eyes and let myself pitch into the flow of magic between us. Even as he moved inside me, his storm danced in my flesh, and my magic bloomed in his own chest.

"Alyx," he gasped.

"Kelvar," I echoed back, my voice a broken sob as I hurtled toward the edge.

Our pleasure crested together, reverberating back and forth in our magic in endless waves until nothing was left but sparks skittering over our skin. We gasped for breath as I managed to open my eyes, meeting Kelvar's as he pressed his forehead to my own.

We stayed like that for long minutes. When Kelvar did eventually pull his length from me and arrange us on our sides, he kept his forehead pressed to mine.

"Forever," he said, unprompted. "I built this city for you to last forever. And our love will last even longer. Even in eternity, I will not be parted from you."

I smiled, wrapping my arms around his shoulders and pulling him close. I did not doubt his power to make it so.

"I look forward to eternity."

Continue the legend of Kelvadan and The Ballan Desert in BLOOD OF THE SANDS.

An exile desperate for belonging. A masked warlord doomed by the magic in his blood. A bond that could save the Ballan Desert—or destroy the world as they know it.

ALSO BY

The Ballan Desert
Blood of the Sands
Crown of the Dunes

The Talented Fairy Tales Trilogy
Beauty and the Blade
Little Red Shadow
The Hood and His Thief

Defenders of the Light
Monsters in the Museum
Chaos and Crowns

ACKNOWLEDGEMENTS

This story would not exist without my good friend, Megan Van Dyke, who designed the beautiful cover for this book and was an invaluable sounding board as it was drafted.

Friel, my editor, deserves so much praise and recognition. She is the unsung hero of all of my books, and the most incredible cheerleader every step of the way.

All of my author friends, thank you for sticking with me through the good times, the bad, and the just plain weird. Lily, you are truly a once-in-a-lifetime kind of friend. You deserve the world.

And last but most certainly not least, to my family. You are my entire world.

ABOUT THE AUTHOR

S.C. Grayson has been reading fantasy novels since she was a little girl, and that has developed into a love of writing and storytelling. She is currently focused on fantasy and paranormal romance.

When she is not sitting in a local coffee shop writing and consuming an iced americano, Grayson is a nurse researcher with a focus on breast cancer genetics. She lives in Chicago with her loving husband and their two cats, who enjoy contributing to her work by walking across her keyboard at inopportune moments (the cats, not the husband).